Ben Franklin's War

Also by Stephen Eaton Hume

Midnight on the Farm
Rainbow Bay
Red Moon Follows Truck
A Miracle for Maggie
Frederick Banting: Hero, Healer, Artist

Ben Franklin's War

Stephen Eaton Hume

A SANDCASTLE BOOK
A MEMBER OF THE DUNDURN GROUP
TORONTO

Editor: Michael Carroll
Design: Jennifer Scott
Printer: Webcom

Library and Archives Canada Cataloguing in Publication

Hume, Stephen Eaton, 1947-
Ben Franklin's war / Stephen Eaton Hume.

ISBN-10: 1-55002-638-0
ISBN-13: 978-1-55002-638-2

1. Franklin, Benjamin, 1706-1790--Juvenile fiction. I. Title.

PS8565.U556B45 2006 jC813'.54 C2006-904610-7

1   2   3   4   5   10   09   08   07   06

Conseil des Arts du Canada   **Canada Council for the Arts**   Canada   ONTARIO ARTS COUNCIL CONSEIL DES ARTS DE L'ONTARIO

We acknowledge the support of the **Canada Council for the Arts** and the **Ontario Arts Council** for our publishing program. We also acknowledge the financial support of the **Government of Canada** through the **Book Publishing Industry Development Program** and **The Association for the Export of Canadian Books**, and the **Government of Ontario** through the **Ontario Book Publishers Tax Credit program**, and the **Ontario Media Development Corporation**.

Printed and bound in Canada.
Printed on recycled paper.

www.dundurn.com

Dundurn Press
3 Church Street, Suite 500
Toronto, Ontario, Canada
M5E 1M2

Gazelle Book Services Limited
White Cross Mills
High Town, Lancaster,
England
LA1 4XS

Dundurn Press
2250 Military Road
Tonawanda, NY
U.S.A. 14150

TABLE OF CONTENTS

ACKNOWLEDGEMENTS

I wish to thank the following people: Taiaiake Alfred, Kanien'kehaka (Mohawk) scholar at the University of Victoria, for his guidance; Niko Silvester, owner of the White Raven Bookbindery; Trisha Telep, who helped edit the original manuscript; Cathie Garvin, a sign-language teacher who taught me much; and Michael Carroll, the intrepid editorial director at The Dundurn Group. Any flaws in the manuscript are mine.

PREFACE

History tells us that Benjamin Franklin journeyed to Canada in late March and early April 1776 when he was seventy years old. He went on foot, by carriage, and by boat. Although he was unusually vigorous for a man of his age, the trip nearly killed him. His mission was to persuade the Canadians to join the Thirteen Colonies against the British, but when he arrived he knew that his task was a lost cause. He was forced to return to the Colonies where he assisted in the preparation of the Declarion of Independence. Later that year he was sent on a mission to France to secure French aid and to help chart America's course through the Revolutionary War.

Franklin was a great inventor and one of the most famous thinkers of the Enlightenment. What if the great man had used his knowledge of electricity and air currents to travel to Canada by balloon, seven years earlier than the first manned flights in Paris? *Ben Franklin's War* is history imagined, a parallel universe to the "recorded" history we accept as true. It is not a *roman à clef*. It is something Franklin would have admired: a work of the imagination.

If the novel fits anywhere, it probably belongs to the steampunk genre. Steampunk fiction, set in earlier periods of history, features advanced inventions and devices that employ primitive technology. Above all, *Ben Franklin's War* is a story about Franklin and a precocious teenage rebel — both in their own way struggling to be free of tyranny.

Ben Franklin's War
Being an Account of Courage, Bloodshed, and the Search for the Legendary Fly-Fishing River of Brandywine

What matters deafness of the ear, when the mind hears. The one true deafness, the incurable deafness, is that of the mind.

— Victor Hugo

Eripuit caelo fulmen sceptrumque tyrannis.
He seized the lightning from the heavens and the sceptre from the tyrants.

— A.R.J. Turgot

CHAPTER I

I Introduce Myself and Beg Your Indulgence

My name is Michael Flynn, and I have been Deaf for as long as I can remember. I am writing this with a Canada goose quill (some of the feathers are missing) and a bottle of homemade ink. Please excuse where the ink has splashed from my pen. I would not be telling you this story except I rode in an airship with the great inventor Ben Franklin, and watched men die in battle, and surveyed the stars, all in the space of a week. You may wonder how a fourteen-year-old boy living in Quebec City met the Rebel Franklin. I will tell you, but first I will list some particulars about myself.

I live in an orphanage, St. Francis of Assisi Home for Foundlings, close by the River St. Lawrence. I own three books, a fishing rod, and a box of treasures. One of my best friends is White Dog. He was raised by wolves. His skin is an unearthly white, and he has a shaved head with pictures of animals tattooed on his skull. My other best friend is Madeline. She is Deaf, like me, and lives in the girls' part of the orphanage. My favourite teacher is Brother Jean, who believes in

Good Works. My enemy is Brother Nessus, who threatens me with the Cauldron of Hell.

My Books:

I. *The Compleat Angler or the Contemplative Man's Recreation* by Izaak Walton.
II. *The Pilgrim's Progress* by John Bunyan.
III. *Experiments and Observations on Electricity* by Benjamin Franklin.

My Fishing Rod:

Bamboo from the Isle of Japan, with a whale-bone extension and a brass reel.

My Treasures:

I. A bottle of "sympathetic stain," otherwise known as invisible ink, for writing spy letters.
II. Equipment for making flies: head feathers from a mallard drake (they shine in the Sun and attract fish); blue yarn; hair from a horse's mane; wool from a black sheep; silk from one of Cook's shawls; thread; fish hooks; scissors; pliers for bending wire; wax, to finish the flies; a spindle of horsehair fishing line; assorted surgeon's tools I found in a field where the limbs of the grievously wounded were amputated.
III. A bottle of black homemade ink upon which I have affixed a label, "Never Ending," because

that is how long it is taking me to write this book.

IV. A pocket watch with no hands.

V. Seven musket balls melted down and pierced for fishing weights.

VI. A Mohawk knife and scabbard decorated with porcupine quills. I use the knife to sharpen the nib of my writing quill and to clean the fish I catch.

Writing and fishing. What more do I need? Let us begin.

CHAPTER II

An Eclipse of the Moon

The night I met Ben Franklin there was an eclipse of the Moon. The wind came from the south. The English writer Izaak Walton said: "When the wind is south,/It blowes your bait into a fishes mouth."

It was April 2, 1776, my fourteenth birthday, and all I wanted to do was go fishing. I used a special fly for fishing at night. It looked like a silver moth. The trout flew out of the water like birds just to taste it.

I wondered how high the fish would jump in an eclipse. I cursed my luck that on a night like this I had been ordered to stay inside. All the orphans had. There was a curfew on account of the war with the American Rebels who were camped outside the city. Brother Jean made me swear a solemn promise to stay inside. He knew how much I liked fishing at night.

So there I was scrubbing pots in the kitchen with Cook. Out the window I had a good view of the river, the Bridge of Ghosts, and the gravestones in the cemetery. The river went almost dry in summer, but in the spring runoff when the snow melted it was a flood.

Around here we called it River No River. I watched the shadow of the Earth creep slowly across the Moon.

Cook turned to me. "Michael, something strange is going to happen tonight."

"Strange?" I shaded my eyes. This meant *strange* or *hidden*. I communicated with Cook by reading her lips and talking in home signs, a kind of language of hand gestures that most people in the orphanage understood.

"Like the end of the world strange," she said. "The animals are confused. Look yonder by the barn. See?"

A doe was grazing near the paddock. Every so often she would rise and walk a few halting steps on her hind legs. The plough horse was dancing around the corral on his back legs, too.

Lightning flashed. The doe fled into the trees. And there was thunder. I felt the reverberations in my fingertips. I can tell the difference between musket or cannon fire, the tread of a mouse, or the roll of thunder. *This* was thunder.

"Out!" Cook screamed. She rushed to the kitchen door that had been left ajar. A red rooster had strutted into the kitchen and was leaping around in circles. "Get out before I make you into a stew!" Cook yelled at him.

And, I thought to myself, *before I pluck your tail feathers to make a pretty fly*.

She shooed the bird out and slammed the door.

"What are you making?" I signed.

"Applesauce cake," Cook said. She signed, "It feels like the dead want to come out of their graves tonight." Then she stoked the stove.

Cook was African. She was a slave once. Imagine. What was it like to be bought and sold like an animal?

She escaped from Virginia by way of a Maryland plantation in Charles County. As a slave, she planted and cut tobacco. She knew everything there was to know about tobacco. Cook had book learning and religion, too, and as much superstition as her soul could bear. She lived in the attic of the orphanage.

One time, White Dog and I sneaked into her room. We saw an altar, a figure made of corncobs, and a candle that sputtered in its drippings. The room smelled sweet and spicy, like cinnamon and beeswax. Cook was standing before the altar wearing a strange robe. She had stripes painted on her face. She did not see us because she was chanting and her eyes were closed. We were frightened most to death and left as fast as we could. But I still loved her so. Sometimes she was scarier than the Evil One, and that was why the Evil One stayed away from her.

CHAPTER III

My Parents

I was born in Quebec around the year 1762. In which village, I didn't know. I remembered sitting on my mother's lap in front of a stone fireplace and looking out the window at the snow falling the way leaves from a tree dropped quietly on a river.

I remembered the silence.

I remembered my mother and father praying over me, but I could not recall their faces. I remembered that my father used to hit me with a leather belt, as if he could drive out the demon that had seized my tongue. I remembered the welts, and how they burned like the stings of wasps.

When it was clear I could neither hear nor speak, I was given to a stranger, a man with a long black beard. How old was I? Maybe four or five. I did not remember my mother or father saying goodbye. I was hoisted onto a horse. I was not afraid: I thought I was going for a ride. The stranger sat behind me. He smelled of wood smoke and linseed oil. We rode for a long time. The sky was dark with snow clouds when we finally stopped. The stranger hauled me off the horse, gently took my hand, walked me into the heart of the forest, and left me there to die.

He walked away, and the forest swallowed him. I sat under a tree and searched my pockets for food, but found nothing. It began to snow. Suddenly, a wolf appeared. The hackles stood up along her back. She curled her body around mine and I slept. I dreamed the animal's dreams — hunters, spears stained with blood, the taste of cold metal.

Sometime near dawn the wolf disappeared. The Sun came up, but the rays did not warm me. I stood, rubbed my arms, and began to walk. I walked to keep warm. I was determined not to die. Finally, I saw a road through the trees. A wagon passed by. A Brother was in it, a servant of the Creator. Hearing my pitiful howls, he stopped and wrapped a blanket that smelled of horses around me and carried me to the buckboard. His name was Brother Jean, and he gave me a drink of water from his flagon. His face was scarred with smallpox, but to me it seemed flawless. I leaned against him, and the motion of the carriage rocked me to sleep.

Surely I was lucky to be alive. But was it luck or the position of the stars? Brother Jean believed I must have been born on the night of an eclipse and that I would lead a charmed life. Some people believe that stars and planets can cause bad things to happen to people and that an eclipse of the Moon is when the Moon is eaten by witches and the only way to make the demons go away is to light firecrackers and beat on pots and pans. People believe all kinds of crazy things. Brother Jean says the planets are good and that the stars are good to me. I believe him. I am fortunate, considering other Deaf people are forgotten or chained up in asylums.

I was taken to the home for foundlings where Brother Jean taught literature and astronomy. He disregarded the common opinion, based on the writings of St. Augustine, that you were damned to eternal pain unless you could actually *hear* the Word of God.

It was Brother Jean who taught me to home-sign, a pantomime of hand gestures used by the Deaf to communicate. White Dog and Madeline understood the signs, as did Cook and a few of our neighbours, but to outsiders it was a foreign language. Brother Nessus refused to learn to home-sign. He claimed it was a tool of the Devil. Home-signing was my language the way English or French was the language of other people. Deafness was an affliction only to those who could hear. Once, in the barn, when we were sawing wood, Brother Jean explained it to me.

"Think of words as those small blocks of wood. Think ... words ... blocks ..." he signed. "When we speak, we set the blocks in a row, but when we sign, the blocks are the shapes made by our hands, stacked on top of one another, and that is also a kind of language."

I remembered the night Brother Jean took me outside and taught me my first word. *Snow.* Soon I had home signs for *hurt*, *love*, *dogs*, *cats*, *cows*, *fields*, *rivers*, *fish*, and *fly-fishing*. In the beginning I could only express my simplest thoughts and feelings. Later I began to sign complex words, phrases, and sentences. And all this time Brother Jean was teaching me to read, too. I began to read books about the saints and the joys of trout fishing. I read about Ben Franklin and his theories about planets, tides, and the magic of electricity.

The orphanage was a modest house of stone and wood paled by the wind and sunlight. Next door was a stone cottage where the girls lived with Ursuline nuns. The girls were taught sewing and reading and made the clothing for all the orphans. The boys were taught farming and carpentry. We wore brown shirts and pants; the girls wore indigo dresses. The orphanage was my home. It was an island surrounded by farmers, merchants, and Indians. The farmers and merchants were of French and English descent. The Indians, mostly Algonquin and Iroquois, had lived in this country since time had begun. The Huron were wiped out in the smallpox epidemic before I was born. Brother Nessus was afraid of the Indians. He did not want to be tortured, he said. I wondered if I would go to the Bad Place because I wished the Indians would capture him.

Our chapel was built with stones from the river, and we had sermons there on the nature of Hell, which was like British North America, only hotter, with suffering that lasted an eternity. Brother Nessus knew a lot about Hell. He said that White Dog and I were going there.

After chapel was breakfast. A potbellied stove threw off smoke but not much comfort. We ate at six long oak tables and sang grace before each meal. (I said it silently.) The pine benches were the same sort as the ones we used in chapel, which gave me the feeling of eating when I should be praying and praying when I should be eating. Breakfast was fried bread or biscuits, tea, and milk. Dinner was thin soup and more bread. On special occasions we might have corn fritters, ham, chicken, and maple syrup. Leftovers went to the stronger, older boys.

Such was life in an orphanage. Some of the boys were cruel and threw rocks at the dogs and horses.

We had two barns, a corral, a vegetable garden, a corn patch, and a smokehouse for curing hams. The barns had false windows painted on them, complete with stars and moons. Madeline was a good artist, so Brother Jean let her paint all the false windows. The windows were meant to fool bad spirits and witches. When witches tried to fly through the windows to spoil the crops or make the animals sick, they crashed into the walls.

The cemetery was where the Brothers were buried, along with some orphans and a few poor folks from the city. Some of the gravestones had lightning rods attached to prevent the reanimation of corpses. I told Cook I had never seen a dead person come back to life. "See," she whispered, "the lightning rods *work*."

The stones that made me the saddest were for the infants. Their headstones were decorated with little carved cherubs. Cook said the ghosts walked to the river from the cemetery and stood on the bridge to gaze at the water. That was why people called it the Bridge of Ghosts. A boy from the orphanage tried to run away one night and crossed the bridge. To this day no one knew what had happened to him, not even Brother Jean. I was not afraid of ghosts. As I said, I had fished the river at night and had seen strange white mists and ghostly shapes hanging above the water. Why be afraid? At these times I just repeated to myself: *I am Michael Flynn and I am afraid of nothing.*

Sometimes if I had trouble going to sleep at night I silently recited to myself the poems of John Donne or Andrew Marvell and lulled myself with the rolling words.

One of my favourite prose passages to recite in the dark was from *The Compleat Angler*:

> But I will lay aside my Discourse of Rivers, and tell you some things of the Monsters, or Fish, call them what you weill, that they breed and feed in them. Pliny the philosopher says (in the third Chapter of his ninth Book) that in the Indian Sea, the Fish call'd the Balaena or Whirle-pool, is so long and broad, as to take up more in length and breadth than two Acres of ground, and of other Fish of two hundred cubits long: and that in the river Ganges, there be Eeles of thirty foot long. He says there, that these Monsters appear in that Sea only, when the tempestuous winds oppose the Torrents of Waters falling from the rocks into it, and so turning what lay at the bottom to be seen on the waters top. And he says, that the people of Cadara (an island near this place) make the Timber for their houses of those Fish-bones. He there tells us, that there are sometimes a thousand of these great Eeles found wrapt, or interwoven together. He tells us there, that it appears that Dolphins love musick, and will come, when call'd for, by some men or boys, that know and use to feed them, and that they can swim as swift as an Arrow can be shot out a Bow; and much of this is spoken concerning the Dolphin, and other Fish ...

And in the dark, in the deep dark of just-before-sleep, I listed the names of the wondrous fish and other creatures that might be seen today, the words flashing in my head like lightning: *Hog-Fish, Dog-Fish, Cony-Fish, Parrot-Fish, Shark, Poyson-Fish, Salamander, Sea Snake …*

I did not find it hard to memorize words. Once, Brother Jean told me the Deaf were thought to have no memory and, therefore, no reason or intelligence. I could tell you that was a lie.

Brother Jean had a small observatory at the back of the orphanage where he looked at the stars. He kept his library there, too, full of wonderful books on stars and planets, books by the inventor Benjamin Franklin. Sometimes I sneaked into the observatory late at night to look at the stars and read about wonders. I was particularly fond of a beautiful gilt-edged, leather-bound volume called *Mysterious Secrets of the Anglers*. This book talked about a river named Brandywine where the fish were white and had pale eyes because they lived most of their lives in underground limestone caverns.

I memorized passages from *Mysterious Secrets of the Anglers* and added these to my nightly recitations. Did you know the Brandywine could appear mysteriously at the base of a mountain or even in someone's house, driving the inhabitants into the street and turning the street into a river? There was no map in the book, though — no map *anywhere* for that matter, showing Brandywine on it. All I had to go on were legends and fables. Some people in the book said that Brandywine could only be found in the place of every person's greatest desire. To find the river, they said, you had to trust your heart. It was my dream to fish Brandywine one day with both White Dog and Madeline. All three of us — together.

Brother Jean taught me how to fly-fish in winter during a snowstorm when the normally elusive rainbow trout had lost their skill. He also taught me to fish at night when the big fish came out of their holes and hunted for moths and careless spirits. Sometimes, Brother Jean said, a fish would swallow a spirit and then become wily and strong. He taught me to believe in myself and told me I was a perfect child of the Creator the way I was and not an aberration to be abandoned in the woods or locked in an asylum. I learned about the heavens and the poets of the seventeenth century from him, the stars, the mystics, and the scientific marvels of Benjamin Franklin, that ingenious colonial inventor whose pamphlet *Experiments and Observations on Electricity* introduced the lightning rod and made him famous overnight.

CHAPTER IV

Dead People

Cook gave me a piece of the applesauce cake when it was done and wished me a happy birthday, but she made me promise to go straight to bed and not sneak out to fish. "It's too dangerous tonight," she said. "The soldiers will shoot you."

The British Redcoats were everywhere. New France had fallen in 1760, and ever since then it had been nothing but war. So I climbed the stairs, went into my room, and sat on the bed. I ate my cake in the dark and watched the Moon and the unfolding eclipse. I jotted down some observations in my journal the way Brother Jean always encouraged me to do.

Lunar Eclipse: April 2, 1776

The Moon is a strange reddish colour like a penny. It is a glowing copper ball in the sky. Every so often there is a lightning flash and a flurry of snow. Cook is right. Something strange is going to happen.

Even so, I was determined to go fishing. Solar eclipses could end in seven minutes, but an eclipse of the Moon could take several hours, and I wanted to see if the fish were biting. Cook worried too much. If it wasn't soldiers, it was Boo Hags. She was right about one thing. The fighting was bloody.

In November last year the American Richard Montgomery captured Montreal from the British. In December Montgomery's soldiers joined with Benedict Arnold's forces, which had marched overland from the Maine coast to Quebec. Together, between the hours of four and six on the morning of December 31, they attacked Quebec City. The battle was a disaster for the Americans. Arnold was wounded, and Montgomery was killed by a lethal volley of cannon and musket fire. The Americans met with unexpected hostility from British soldiers and armed citizens of Quebec. The Rebels lay bloody all over the streets and alleys of Lower Town. I saw the corpses with my own eyes.

The American troops were half-starved. Hundreds of American soldiers were taken prisoner by the British and confined in the town's seminary. They were allowed fresh air and exercise but no pens or paper. (I cannot imagine being forbidden to write. I would go mad.) The remaining American troops who were not killed or captured or who did not die of disease or exposure were camped now on the plains outside the city's walls. They were desperate. Brother Nessus, a Loyalist, had said, with a smile on his face, that two Rebel mercenaries were arrested the other day for stealing a goose from a farmer and were hanged.

The British troops were waiting for the Americans to attack again. Everywhere you looked there was war. Someone was nailing up posters on walls and trees, signed by General George Washington, the commander of the American army:

> After all, are we not one people?
> Who are the British but our masters?
> Was it not European soil we fled
> when we came to this land to seek our freedom?

I did not know which side I was on and did not really care. I just wanted to fish. The war did not interest me the same way as, say, a fat salmon or a flapping rainbow trout. It was not my problem that the Americans and the British could not get along, was it?

I glanced at my new fly-fishing rod that was leaning against the wall. It was my birthday gift from Brother Jean. It had an actual reel and was made of bamboo directly from Japan. I had never seen such a luxury. I was used to cutting a length of willow branch, tying horse-hair line to the end of the pole, and simply casting the line out in water where I thought the fish would rise.

As I finished the last of my cake, I remembered how good it felt to whip the line back and forth in the air to dry the fly. It had been a week since I had last gone fishing, and now it all came back to me — the coolness of standing knee-deep in water, the beauty of the river, watching the line snap out into the wind when the water was troubled and the fish were biting. Most of all, the sensation of a silence that was not only my Deafness but the utter stillness of nature.

I thought of Madeline and White Dog and wished they could sneak out with me. I had taught them how to fly-fish. White Dog, though, did not care for fishing with a pole. He would rather wait in the water and scoop the salmon out with his hands. He had a liking for raw fish.

White Dog and I were about the same age. He slept outside in the barn on account of he was what Brother Jean called a "wild child." The Brothers tried to civilize him, but it was no use. He slept during the day and went out hunting at night. He liked the taste of raw meat and fresh blood but ate other things, too. I introduced him to roasted potatoes, but he liked them best when they were only partially cooked and covered with ash. He also ate beech and hickory nuts, berries, roots, wild onions, and roasted corn. Sometimes he ate in the dining room with the other boys, but that was rare. If we had corn for dinner, White Dog would hide a few uneaten cobs in his shirt and bury them outside. He had a secret cache of food somewhere in the woods and a cave along River No River.

White Dog loved to hunt. Because of this, Brother Jean let him help at slaughtering time. He was good at killing chickens with a swift bite to the neck and at killing the hogs with a knife, too. Brother Jean always gave him a pint of fresh pig's blood for his labour. Sometimes Brother Nessus slaughtered the hogs, but they ran away from him and squealed mightily when he chased them around the corral. It was eerie the way they seemed to stay calm when White Dog was there.

Brother Nessus did not want White Dog and me to sit together in class because he said we were bad influences on each other. To him, White Dog was just an *animal*.

Brother Nessus did not like me to sign my words, either, and always tried to make me speak.

"Say *O! O!* Say *Mo! Mo!* Say Moses was a baby!" Brother Nessus yelled, his face red as a beet. "Michael! Flynn! You! Sinful! Unrepentant! Loafer! Speak!" He tried to pry open my mouth and grab my tongue, seizing my face with both hands and forcing me to watch his mouth when he pronounced the vowels and consonants. But I would squeeze my eyes shut. I hated him! Sometimes, when we were fighting like this, White Dog would growl at Brother Nessus and he, afraid for his safety, would release me.

I looked out my window at the Moon. How many times had it felt the shadow of the Earth move across its face in an eclipse just like this one? I wondered about what Cook had said about the world of the living and the world of the dead. Brother Jean said Madeline was going to be adopted soon. Eliza Fisk, a wealthy widow in town, was going to be her mother. Mrs. Fisk had already signed the adoption papers. Madeline had only one more day left in the orphanage. I hoped to see her before she left.

At the end of the hall Brother Nessus sat in his room reading the Bible by a three-candled lantern. My door was open, and I saw the reflection of the flames playing on the hallway ceiling. My guess was that his feet rested on his gout stool. Brother Nessus had the gout because he drank too much wine. That was why he walked with a cane. His custom was to finish reading, sit in his musician's chair, and play the violoncello angrily for a few minutes. Then, and only then, would he climb into bed and fall asleep.

I waited for about an hour after Brother Nessus had extinguished his candles and gone to sleep before I put on my clothes. I stuffed a quilt under my blanket to make it appear I was asleep, then slipped on my deerskin vest with all my favourite flies attached in rows. When I needed one, say, a Black Widow or a Silver Moth, I just plucked it off and tied it to my line. I pulled my fur hat over my ears and buttoned my wool overcoat. In the inside pocket of the coat was my ragged copy of *The Pilgrim's Progress*. I kept it there so I could look at the pictures and read about monsters. Sometimes Cook would read it aloud to me, but she would have to read slowly and carefully because reading lips was not as easy as you might think. There were many words that sounded different but looked the same when they came out of your mouth.

I tiptoed down the hall so the floorboards would not creak and wake Brother Nessus. I was almost out the front door when I bumped into Cook.

"Michael Flynn!" She shook her head. "One of these days you're going to drive me crazy." There was flour on her hands, and it fell to the floor in clouds as she wagged her finger at me. "Where do you think you're going?" But she knew just by looking at my fishing rod what I was planning. She shook her head again and signed that I should be careful.

"There are spirits out tonight," she said. "I can feel them. An eclipse of the Moon makes a hole in the sky where the spirits fall to Earth." She took a bottle filled with sewing pins out of her apron pocket, opened the front door, and set it outside on the steps. "If there's a Witch Hag, it always stops to count the pins and then you can make your escape."

She crossed herself three times, and I put my arms around her. I loved her. I made her swear to the powers that be not to tell the Brothers I had left.

CHAPTER V

Freedom

Freedom! I stuck out my tongue and tasted the snow. It was a pretty night, all right. The sky was mostly clear, so I figured the snow must be blowing in from the sea. Through the clouds I could see the Big Dipper and the North Star. Somewhere a sailor was guiding his voyage by that star.

I walked down to the river and stood on the Bridge of Ghosts. Every so often there would be a flash of lightning. I thought I could see ghosts walking among the gravestones in the cemetery. Ghosts or soldiers. Sometimes it seemed they were one and the same, they were both so intimate with death.

A hand touched my shoulder.

It was a man. His eyes looked hollow and he had the mark of Death upon him. Somehow I knew that he would soon die. He had on a torn black beaver hat and a long threadbare coat. He could not have been warm on such a freezing night. I reckoned he was a Rebel. A Redcoat would not have been caught dead dressed so poorly. His moustache was smeared with frozen snot, his feet were wrapped in rags, and he carried a musket and a flask of propellant powder slung over his shoulder. Brother Nessus said the Evil One himself walked at night. Brother Nessus should know.

The man asked me why the town was so quiet. I pretended I did not understand and pointed to my ears.

"Deaf?"

I nodded.

"You look harmless enough. You a waif? Got no home? All you Canadians must be asleep or too drunk to fight." He turned and spat. The saliva froze when it hit the snow.

"When we left New York," he continued, "we was three thousand men. General Arnold was our leader and we loved him. Would have followed him to Hell. But this is worse than Hell!" He wiped his nose. "The same wind blows in New England, but not this cold! Now we number only a few hundred. Some of us have deserted or died of disease or from this infernal cold. The rest of us wait for the war to be over." His buckshot eyes stared blindly into the distance. "I just want to go home. Drink a bottle of rum. Forget."

The Rebel blew on his fingers and began to load his musket. The weapon was almost as tall as I was. I reckoned the barrel alone was almost four feet long.

"The British will never surrender. Lexington and Concord, that was one thing." He shook his head. "The British army made an easy target for our snipers. They marched in straight lines in red uniforms! How could you miss them?" He laughed. "Now we're fighting a lost cause. How do we expect to invade Canada when we can't even kick the British off colonial soil?"

He stared at me, and I shivered again. The loaded gun was in his hand. I held my breath waiting to see what he was going to do. Was he crazy enough to shoot me?

"Well, good night, Dumb Boy." The American slung his musket across his shoulder. I watched the poor fellow trudge off in the snow, still dreaming of home.

I had dropped my fishing rod in the snow during all the excitement. Now I picked it up and marched down the other side of the bridge to the clearing that led to my favourite bank to fish from at night. It was a special spot where the big fish settled after the Sun went down. And, yes, I meant to go fishing. I was not scared away that easily.

The Moon was still in eclipse. Perfect! I might have twenty minutes left if I was lucky. I recalled something Ben Franklin wrote about eclipses in *Poor Richard's Almanack*:

Some of these Eclipses foreshow great Grief and many Tears. War we shall have too much of, for all Christians have not yet learn'd to love one another. I Pray Heaven defend these Colonies from every Enemy, and give them Bread enough, Peace enough, Money enough, and plenty of good Cyder.

Hell and damnation!

I spotted three more Rebel soldiers and ducked behind a tree. They were taking long swigs from a bottle. "They don't know who they're dealing with, boys." One of the soldiers wobbled unsteadily on his feet. "I'll rip 'em limb from limb!" The other two Americans laughed and passed the bottle between them.

I managed to sneak out of there without being seen and get across the bridge again. How do you like that? No question about it. There would surely be no fishing tonight unless I wanted to be used for target practice. And I certainly did not. But I was not tired and I did not want to go back to the orphanage and listen to Brother Nessus snoring like a pig blowing bubbles in the mud — he was so loud I could feel the vibrations. So, in the end, I decided to walk to the smokehouse and do some reading. It was a decision that would change my life.

The smokehouse was a little stone shed near the main building of the orphanage. Like our barn, the smokehouse had a painting of an open window with false ivy growing around the frame. I liked going there to read and be alone. There was always enough light from the one real window or, if it was dark, from the coals. It was warm, and I liked the way it smelled. On a sunny day, the warped glass window made the trees and hills seem as if they were underwater. I settled down against the back wall of the smokehouse, and by the light of the coals I began to read from my tattered copy of *The Pilgrim's Progress*:

> When they entered upon this valley, they thought that they heard a groaning as of dead men; a very great groaning. They thought also, that they did hear words of lamentation, spoken as of some in extreme torment. These things made the boys quake; the women also looked pale and wan. But their guide bid them be of further comfort.

So they went on a little farther, and they thought that they felt the ground begin to shake under them, as if some hollow place was there. They heard also a kind of hissing, as of serpents; but nothing as yet appeared. Then said the boys, "Are we not yet at the end of this doleful place?"

Now, remember when I said I was not afraid of anything? Well, it was true. Most of the time. But there, in the smokehouse, as I read about the lamentation of the dead, I felt something close to fear. I remembered what Cook had said about witches, and I prayed that if there was a Hag around she was still counting the pins.

I read through my book trying to find a cheerful passage. When I caught myself yawning, I knew it was time to get to bed before anyone at the orphanage woke up and missed me. I returned my book to the inside pocket of my coat and stood to leave.

That was when it happened.

The glass window of the shed exploded, and I was knocked to the floor. My chest felt as if someone had struck my heart with a hammer. I could not breathe. My mind raced. *A witch has flown into the smokehouse! I am dying! This is it! I am going to die!*

Then I realized that I had been shot.

I opened my jacket to check for blood. Instead of a wound, however, I found a musket ball lodged in my copy of *The Pilgrim's Progress* — in the letter *g* of *Pilgrim*, as a matter of fact. I plucked out the lead, and I am not ashamed to say, kissed the book in gratitude for saving my life.

When I stepped outside, I saw British soldiers on the hill firing at a group of Rebels who had penetrated the city. The regiment had been waiting for the Americans on high ground in the falling snow.

The man leading the Rebels raised his sword and fell in a barrage of British fire. The Redcoats tumbled forward in the snow stopping only to measure powder and shot for their muskets. For a moment, all I could see were flashes of steel, bursts of musket flame, and clouds of rolling smoke. A red tide of British soldiers swept down the hill. Behind them, more soldiers shot arrows tipped with blazing rosin and brimstone at the Americans. The arrows trailed fire across the sky and landed on the Rebel wagons, igniting them in an instant.

I ran for my life across the snow and freezing mud and stumbled over the legs of a dead Rebel, not much older than I, wearing a paper pennant with the word *Freedom* emblazoned across it. Then I saw him. The man I had met on the Bridge of Ghosts. He had been skewered through with a sword, and snow blew into the cavern of his open, toothless mouth. I figured he had died in the middle of another speech.

As fast as I could, I hid behind a smouldering freight wagon. All around me soldiers were running, shooting, swinging their sabres. Someone grabbed me so hard I thought my arm would break. A British soldier with epaulets and braid beneath his greatcoat shook me and shouted. I pointed to my ears and signed, "Spare me, I am Deaf," but he struck me across the face with his pistol stock. I fell to my knees and prayed for my life the way Brother Jean had taught me.

Our. Right hand swept across chest.
Father. Hands placed just above stomach.
In Heaven. Hands raised skywards.

The soldier cocked his pistol and aimed it between my eyes as I prayed. You noticed the strangest things when you were about to die: gold leaf on the barrel of the pistol, silver inlay on the stock, satyrs and fawns.

Hallowed be thy Name …

The pistol exploded in a flash of light. I reckoned the gunpowder must have frozen or the barrel had filled with ice, because he tossed aside the shattered weapon and pulled his sabre from its scabbard to finish me off. The sword had blood on it. He held it above me with both hands. Then something remarkable happened. He looked up.

I looked up, too. My eyes swam from the gunpowder flash, but I was sure I saw his lips form one word — "Comet!"

But it was not a comet. It was a basket attached to a balloon flying above the trees in the falling snow. Glowing glass containers were strung around the basket on a chain. It looked like a star as it blinked and floated over the city. The lighted containers were growing dim, and the ship seemed to be losing altitude in a shower of sparks. I saw a man inside, a laughing man wearing spectacles.

CHAPTER VI

I Meet the Great Scientist

The soldier stood there like a fish frozen in torchlight.

I ran, but not in the direction of the orphanage. Instead, I ran towards the forest where the strange airship had mysteriously disappeared. After White Dog, I was the fastest runner at the home for foundlings. I did not look back as I plunged through the deep snow. Brother Jean had told me all about shooting stars and creatures that live on other planets. He had quoted Benjamin Franklin in astronomy class: "If there are any inhabitants in Mars, the Earth and the Moon will appear to them, thro' Telescopes, if they have any such Instruments."

Father Jean read me the poems of St. John of the Cross, a mystic who believed that Time was an illusion and that all Time exists eternally, everywhere, in a single moment of never-ending creation. I might have been afraid of what the dark might hold for me that night, but as I ran into the forest after the airship, I could not contain my excitement. Questions raced through my mind: *When did Time begin? Where was I before I was born? What waits for me in the woods?*

I stopped running and gazed back at the town. The battle fires seemed so small now and the woods were so dark I thought I had passed into the next world. The town flickered in the distance like a burning ship. I sniffed the air. *Smoke.* Far away, through the trees and deeper into the woods, I spotted flames. As I got closer, I could see the airship. It was on fire. Bright orange flames shot up from the ship and licked at the spruce boughs and the trunks of birch trees, curling the white bark. I saw the bespectacled man trying to put out the fire with a blanket. He appeared to be about seventy years of age and was hatless. The top of his head was bald, but straight grey hair fell from the sides to his shoulders. His hair was neither powdered, as was the fashion, nor wigged. He was dressed plainly, like a Quaker, in a long navy blue riding coat.

Gadgets and papers bulged from the large side pockets of his coat. A folding telescope, quill pens, a compass hanging from a leather strap, and a large time-piece on a chain were just some of the objects I spied. The blanket he used to smother the flames had caught fire, and oddly the man was laughing. Tears streamed down his face.

When he saw me, he dropped the blanket in the snow.

"Who goes there!" he said. "Speak!"

I signed that I could not. He seemed intrigued by my hand signs and removed his spectacles — bifocals of his own construction, I learned much later — to wipe away his tears. "Are you a local?" he asked, putting the spectacles back on.

I nodded.

"Loyalist?"

I signed I wasn't sure and shrugged my shoulders.

"Are you a servant of the King?"

I thought of the painting in Brother Nessus's room: King George III. I hated everything about Brother Nessus, so I smashed my fist into my open palm and shook my head.

No. I was not a Loyalist.

"Rebellion against tyranny is obedience to God," the man said. "Help me put out this fire, will you?"

Indeed, the ship continued to burn. I grabbed a large pine bough that had broken off a tree in the crash and worked at extinguishing the flames. Then we both piled snow onto the smouldering ship. That seemed to do the trick.

"It is there!" the man cried, pointing at the sky. "There!" he repeated. "You can see it through the trees."

The Moon was still in shadow. Together we watched the shadow die, and in a few minutes the Moon was born again. The eclipse was over. For a long time, the mysterious gentleman did not speak.

Finally, he turned to me. "Why are you out on such a cold night, friend?"

I motioned to his flying contraption and indicated that I had watched its trajectory into the trees and was compelled to follow it.

"I call it an electric airship," he said proudly. As he adjusted his glasses, I noticed the word *Liberty* painted on the side of the flying machine.

He claimed he spent only eight nights to travel all the way from New York City to Quebec City, faster than boat or carriage, which could take many weeks. To avoid detection, and because the winds were more reliable without the heat waves from the Sun, he flew the ship at night. He seemed to be very taken with this wonderful contraption.

"Pardon me, young man, but you have a nasty burn around your eyes."

I touched the burnt skin with my fingertips. It must have been where the soldier's pistol exploded in my face. Trying to explain what happened to me, I showed him my copy of *The Pilgrim's Progress* with the bullet hole in the *g*.

The man laughed. "You must be a good man if *The Pilgrim's Progress* saved your life. I feel I can trust you. What is your name, my boy?"

"Michael Flynn," I wrote in the snow. "Yours?"

The stranger took a deep breath. "Franklin," he said. "Benjamin Franklin."

The great Franklin! I could not wait to tell Brother Jean! Was he here because of the war? He would be killed if the British got hold of him. Surely Brother Jean would forgive me for breaking curfew now that I had discovered the famous inventor!

Franklin picked up one of the glowing jars from the side of the airship but then dropped it quickly into a snowdrift. He gasped. The jar had burned his hands, for he immediately blew on his fingers to cool them.

"What's that?" I signed, pointing at the fallen jar. I had a million questions to ask.

"I call it a 'wonderful bottle,'" Franklin said. "Technically, it is called a Leyden jar. It stores an electrical charge. The power generated by the electricity turns a propeller mounted at the rear of the ship. The rudder can be moved by a ship's wheel, see?" He moved the rudder side to side. "It was an experiment, really, and not a very successful one at that if you take the crash into account. I have been corresponding with a group of inventors in Paris who are developing balloons for air travel. I envisioned something that would get me closer to the clouds in thunderstorms, and I had this idea that balloons would travel faster using the right air currents, the way sailing ships travel faster on the Gulf Stream. I still think balloons might prove valuable for calculations of the rising and setting of the Sun and Moon and for predicting the weather."

Franklin shook his head. "I could probably get this machine flying again." He pointed up into the trees. "But the fabric balloon, I believe, is beyond repair."

The deflated balloon billowed over the treetops like a giant ghost that wanted to fly but could not.

Franklin found a stub of pencil and half a sheet of notepaper in his pocket. He gave these to me so I could write down what I wanted to say, because he couldn't understand all my home signs.

I wrote, "You are here to map air currents and record the effect of the eclipse on the stars?"

Franklin nodded.

"Your landing here, in Quebec, is just coincidence? Nothing to do with the war?" I scribbled as fast as I could. "With all due respect, Mr. Franklin, I find that hard to believe."

As if we might be spied on, Franklin glanced over his shoulder and then confessed to me the real purpose of his visit. The American Congress had appointed him to be part of a commission to persuade Canada to join the American cause. From the battle scene he had surveyed that evening, I knew he could see this would not be an easy task. The way I saw it, most Canadians just wanted to get on with their lives, never mind the Americans. They wanted to be left alone to run their businesses and farms. This was not Canada's war, they reasoned.

Two other men had been appointed to come to Canada with him. Charles Carroll and Samuel Chase had set out from New York City, and their plan was to sail by sloop up the Hudson River to Lake Champlain and reach Canada, hopefully, by April sometime.

"If Canada joins us, we could be a unified force and expel the British once and for all." Franklin took me over to the ship's basket. "Have you ever seen one of these?" He pulled out a small gadget and explained that it was a reflecting quadrant and was used for navigation. Then he showed me a powerful telescope built by William Herschel, the famous astronomer and stargazer. To me, he seemed much more interested in inventions than in politics. He showed me another queer invention, a tube containing mercury.

"What is that for?" I wrote.

"It is an altimeter," he said.

"Did you invent it?"

"Unfortunately, I did not. It is very wonderful. See, it calculates height by measuring air pressure."

I asked if the altimeter's bad reading was what had caused him to crash.

"No, son," Franklin said. "I could not see in the dark and I struck the top of a pine tree. Some of the Leyden jars exploded and I lost power."

Franklin smiled at me. What a curious-looking man! He had moles on his face and clove-like teeth in need of repair — downright homely. But there was something about him that I liked. I could see that he was a decent, honest man.

Cook was right. Strange days were ahead.

CHAPTER VII

Ben Franklin Becomes Mr. Richard Saunders

It was late. Franklin had been chattering on about flying instruments for what seemed like an hour. Suddenly, I had the feeling we might be watched. I held a finger to my lips. Franklin stopped talking and looked around for any signs of spies. I made the sign of a knife across my throat.

He understood. "Redcoats."

I nodded. We had to be careful. If the British caught him, they would hang us both. I wrote on the paper that he could stay with us in the orphanage. He read the note and thanked me with a short bow. Then we had a look at the airship. It was a sorry sight.

"Why don't we leave the ship in the woods and return for it tomorrow?" Franklin suggested. He tucked his telescope, a few of the more delicate flying instruments, and his flight journal into his huge coat pockets, and we set out for the home for foundlings.

It was snowing lightly as we neared the orphanage and saw the first gruesome signs of the night's battle. Some of the bodies had been carried away, but a few soldiers still lay frozen in the snow. We saw a severed head in a snowdrift, eyes open in surprise. Broken bodies lay across the ground. Redcoat or Rebel, it did not matter. The falling snow would cover all the bodies regardless.

At the orphanage door I rapped once with the heavy brass knocker. The door immediately flew open, and there was Brother Jean. It seemed he had been waiting up for me.

"Where have you been! Have you gone mad? Do you know what time it is, young man? And what is wrong with your face?" Finally, he noticed Franklin. "Who in the world is this?"

"Allow me to introduce myself," Franklin said in perfect French. "Monsieur Benjamin Franklin."

Franklin and I went inside and stood in the hallway. The light from the hall candles glanced off his bifocal spectacles and made him seem like a traveller from another planet.

"I do not believe it," Brother Jean said.

"It is true!" I signed.

Then Brother Jean and Franklin began to speak French. Luckily, I knew French, too, and I even knew how to sign some words in the language. This was one of the first poems I ever learned: *"Arrive la paix, arrive la guerre,/Toujours s'écoule la rivière."* That was a darn sight better than any of the swill Brother Nessus's friend, Captain Pennington, ever wrote. So this was what Brother Jean and Franklin said in the hall.

"You are really Franklin?"

"Yes. It is I."

"When did you arrive?"

"Tonight. I had a long and dangerous journey. Thanks to this boy, Michael Flynn, I am safe."

"Michael Flynn, he always seems to find trouble. He is a rascal and a genius."

"A genius? Do you mean he is crazy about books?"

"No, a fisherman. A genius at fishing. Sometimes he fishes all day and we can't find him. But he is a smart boy, and he will go far in life. He is to be congratulated for saving you."

I was no longer the outlaw who had disobeyed curfew but the one who had discovered the great Benjamin Franklin. Stumbling over Cook's bottle of pins, Brother Jean ushered us into the Great Hall.

We warmed ourselves by the fireplace. Franklin noticed that the room was cold, despite the fire, and offered to make the orphanage a metal insert that would fit in the fireplace and prevent the heat from escaping through the chimney. Brother Jean thanked him for his generosity and commented on the fluency of his French.

Franklin was pleased with himself. "Yes, I have always enjoyed the French language."

Brother Jean was worried Franklin might be arrested. For the duration of his stay at the orphanage, the scientist would be referred to only as "Mr. Richard Saunders," a travelling printer in search of work. Richard Saunders was the pseudonym Franklin used when he wrote his popular monthly gazette, *Poor Richard's Almanack*, which provided the Motions of the Sun and Moon, Useful Tables, and many entertaining Jokes and Jibes. Franklin asked Brother Jean his opinion about the position of Canada in this war. Would Canada consider joining the Americans in their fight against the British?

"I am sympathetic to your cause, Mr. Franklin, but we are not the fourteenth colony," Brother Jean replied. "Both French and English Canadians just want to be left alone. The ordinary citizen on the street wants the fighting to stop."

Franklin shook his head. "We Canadians and Americans are calves from the same cow — Britain. We provide grass to the cow, but the grass is taxed."

"You are too late, my friend. The American army has no choice but to retreat."

Franklin looked desperate. "Please try to understand. To Britain, the colonies are simply British territory. But most of the colonists want to run their own affairs. They want freedom of the press and no government interference. When they rebel, they are shot and their houses are burned. The population of the Thirteen Colonies along the east coast of North America is now more than one and a half million. America is a nation waiting to be born."

"Mr. Franklin, I must counsel you to the fact that your first concern right now should be your own safety. You are surrounded by enemies. One of the Brothers here at the orphanage, Brother Nessus, is a Loyalist. His friend, Arthur Pennington, is the captain of a regiment of the King's soldiers. Another Loyalist in town, Eliza Fisk, publishes pamphlets against the American forces."

"Is that the lady who is adopting Madeline?" I signed to Brother Jean.

"Yes, Michael," he replied. Brother Jean turned to Franklin. "And I should tell you, Mr. Franklin, that Captain Pennington is not only a Redcoat, but he writes excruciatingly bad poetry."

Franklin laughed.

"It is awful!" I signed, and put my hands around my throat as if I were strangling myself. "He says *finny tribe* when he really means *fish*. His poems are full of swamp gas and sentiment."

Brother Jean had had enough of my antics. "You are up far too late, young man. You disobeyed my instructions and put the whole orphanage at risk. I only hope Brother Nessus does not discover you sneaked outside."

Franklin smiled. "I cannot wait to meet this Nessus fellow. He sounds splendid."

"For the moment, he is asleep upstairs. We must keep our voices down and remember to keep your identity a secret." Brother Jean rose out of his armchair. "Let us all get some rest."

Brother Jean showed the great man to his chamber. It had been occupied only a few weeks earlier by a boy who had died of the fever. The first thing Franklin did after Brother Jean had wished him good-night was to open the window and let in the freezing night air. He told me he was not averse to sleeping with the windows open, even in winter. He did not hold to the current belief that night air brings illness and plague, not to mention witches, demons, and Boo Hags.

I hoped no one recognized him tomorrow by the light of day. He was a world-famous scientist and philosopher and a member of the Royal Society. But he was also a leading Rebel. Hanging him as a traitor would be a great victory for the British.

In my journal, I decided I would list his inventions and discoveries:

I.   The theory of plus and minus charges that were at the root of electrical conduction.
II. The kite and key experiment which showed that lightning is electricity.
III. The lightning rod.
IV. Theories about ocean currents, wind currents, and the direction of storms.
V.   The rocking chair and the Philadelphia stove.

I wanted to ask Franklin if I was forgetting anything, but inventions were not on his mind right now. He was sitting on his bed, writing in his notebook with a quill pen. I loaned him my knife to sharpen the quill.

I pointed at his work questioningly.

"I am writing a letter to General Washington," he said. "I have to be careful that this letter does not fall into the wrong hands."

Over his shoulder, I watched him date the letter in black ink: "April 2, 1776." But as soon as the writing appeared on the paper, it disappeared! Franklin saw the look of amazement on my face.

"It is called 'sympathetic stain,'" he said, and showed me the bottle that I had mistaken for simple ink. "It was invented in England by Dr. James Jay. To reveal the words, you simply brush a special restoring fluid on the page. We use this technique for writing letters so the enemy doesn't discover our plans."

As I watched, Franklin began to write an important letter to the American general. The words disappeared one by one off the page in front of him.

"How will you convey this message?" I signed. The quizzical look on my face was all Franklin needed to see to understand me.

"Even in Quebec we have friends," he said. "As soon as I am able, I will pass the letter to a certain dry-goods merchant in Quebec City who will then leave it in a wooden box in a corner of a pre-arranged meadow. At an agreed-upon signal —"

"Signal?" I signed.

"A red cloth tied to a fencepost," he explained. "Once the signal is given, an American operative will pick the letter up from the box and have it delivered by boat across Lake Champlain to the general's headquarters."

There was another question I had been meaning to ask him all night. "Mr. Franklin, are you a spy?"

He was thoughtful for a moment before answering. "Why, yes, Michael. I guess I am."

I could only pray we would not all be hanged.

CHAPTER VIII

We Ride the Airship over the Snow

I woke at five o'clock in the morning to milk the cows. I looked in on Franklin who was still asleep. A light covering of snow lay on his blanket. I washed my face with cold water from a long wooden trough and went downstairs. In the kitchen, Cook was making tea and fried bread.

"Just look at your face!" I guessed she meant the gunpowder burn on my forehead and around my eyes. The wound had started to blister, so Cook took a bottle of green ointment from the cupboard and applied it to my burn. The ointment smelled like Brother Nessus's breath, but I began to feel better almost immediately. She signed that she had made the ointment from an infusion of a species of goldenrod and other wild plants, based upon an Indian recipe.

"I met Benjamin Franklin!" I signed rapidly as she fussed over my burn. "He flew here in an airship and is sleeping upstairs with the window open!"

Cook shrugged. "I am not surprised. I am not surprised by anything anymore." She gave me a chunk of maple sugar and a cup of tea and went back to her work.

I gulped the hot tea, pocketed the sugar, and headed out
to the barn to do my chores.

When I was younger, I did not like milking the
cows. It made my fingers cramp, and I could never get a
good squirt into the pail. But when I got stronger, I
enjoyed it. I liked the sunlight through the slatted roof
and the way the steam rose off the hay in winter. I
sucked on the maple sugar Cook had given me.

As soon as I got to the barn, I saw Madeline. She was
milking a Jersey on the other side of the stable and
glanced up when I entered. Her eyes were blue, like the
dress she wore. Madeline had long black hair that fell to
her waist. She had muscles in her forearms from milking the cows. People said we could be mistaken for
brother and sister.

I got to work and pulled my stool up to lean my
forehead against the cow, breathing in the warm smell
of the animal and watching my pail fill with milk. An
elderly nun in a black habit and white cowl appeared in
the doorway.

"Madeline!" I read her lips. "Madeline!" The nun
waved her hands to get Madeline's attention. "Be
quick!" Then the nun turned and left.

"I couldn't wait to see you!" I signed to Madeline as
she ran to me across the barn.

"Your face looks terrible. What is that smell?"

"A British soldier shot at me last night. Cook put
some kind of ointment on it."

"Michael Flynn, one of these days you are going to
get yourself killed."

"Guess what."

"What?"

"I met Benjamin Franklin last night."

She rolled her eyes. "You expect me to believe that?"

"He's asleep in the dormitory."

"Don't tell tall tales."

"I'm serious, Madeline. It's really him. He flew here in an airship."

"And where is this so-called airship then?"

I did not tell her just then. I motioned her to follow me.

"First, let's go find White Dog."

We found him in the loft of the hay barn eating a partially cooked rabbit. He had sucked the bones clean, and they lay in a pile at his bare feet. White Dog did not like wearing shoes, even in winter. He offered us a rabbit leg.

"That is disgusting," Madeline said.

"I'm giving the skin to Cook to make gloves." He looked at me intently. "What happened to your face?"

I signed to him about my adventures with the soldier, and about Ben Franklin, and about the mysterious airship. But before he would come with us to see the ship, he gathered up the rabbit bones to bury. He would not allow animal bones to be burned or thrown to the dogs. If this were to happen, White Dog told me many times, the souls of the dead animals would be angry and the other animals would not permit themselves to be caught.

It was only two years ago that hunters brought White Dog to the orphanage tangled in a net. There had been talk for some time of a wild boy in the woods, a white boy living like a wolf. I suppose the adults thought they knew what was best so they captured him and brought him to the orphanage. He was a pitiful sight. They figured he had been in the forest for about seven years. When Brother Jean shaved White Dog's long black hair to get rid of his head lice, he discovered the animals tattooed on his skull — a grasshopper, a bear, a trout, and a fox. They were probably inked there by Indians who befriended the wild child at one point in his life in the bush.

The Brothers succeeded in getting White Dog to wear trousers, but he refused to use a knife and fork and rarely took his meals in the dining room. When he was angry, he would close his eyes and strike himself with his fists or weep and cry out. But he could also be very gentle and affectionate. He would not let the Brothers touch him, but I often saw him in Cook's arms, holding her with a sad smile on his face. I gave him the name White Dog. The Brothers gave him another name — John — which he never responded to.

We found the airship in the woods where Franklin and I had left it. Madeline just stared and stared. Some of the Leyden jars still glowed, and White Dog said they buzzed like wasps in a glass. We explored the basket of the ship. I found a folding telescope tucked in a corner, next to a map of Quebec, and we took turns looking at the trees, the distant town, one another. I told White Dog and Madeline never to call Franklin by any other name than Mr. Saunders or we would all be jailed for certain. White Dog was not a problem. It was Madeline I was worried about.

"You know your new mother is a Loyalist," I said. "She even prints pamphlets against the Americans. She would love to hand him over to the Redcoats."

"Stop worrying, Michael. I won't give Franklin away. What do you think I am? A baby? I can keep my mouth shut."

I hoped so, or we were dead.

White Dog, Madeline, and I decided to take the airship back to the orphanage ourselves. We would surprise Franklin! Maybe it could even fly again. We imagined the places we would go. Madeline voted for Paris, France. White Dog had read about Mexico and wanted to go there. I had in mind the legendary river of Brandywine. We gazed at the charred hulk of the magical airship and wished we could fly as far from the St. Francis of Assisi Home for Foundlings as we could. I was jealous of Madeline. She had a new family. She was leaving.

The fabric balloon hung from the top of a tall maple tree. That posed no problem for White Dog, though. He simply climbed up and detached the torn balloon from the branches. It fluttered down like a giant, wounded bird.

"This can be fixed," Madeline said, examining the tear. "Needle and thread are all it will take."

We packed the ripped balloon into the ship and pulled it across the snow to the edge of the woods. Moving the ship took a lot of time and effort. Madeline suggested we slide it down the hill in the general direction of the orphanage. That sounded like a good idea. Besides, we were all worn out.

The three of us pushed with our shoulders to get it going. Madeline jumped in first, then me, then White Dog, who barely made it before the ship was careening down the hill like a speeding toboggan. We ducked under low-hanging branches. The landscape flew by in a blur. What a ride! We were flying! I had never gone this fast before.

We were almost at the bottom of the hill when we hit an icy patch and lost control. The next thing I knew I was lying in the snow on my back next to my friends, laughing. The three of us knew what each other was thinking. *Let's do it again.* But we had to get the ship hidden quickly. It took us only a few more minutes to pull the ship to the barn, park the contraption in one of the stalls, and cover it with straw.

Not long after, Madeline, White Dog, and I lay on the floor in front of the smoky fire in the Great Hall of the orphanage trying to get dry. Our wet clothes hung steaming from hooks on the wall. We took off our boots and wiggled our toes in front of the fire.

Suddenly, White Dog got up and crept over to the door. He was listening to something in the sitting room, and waved us over. We huddled together, the three of us, and peered through the crack in the door to see Brother Nessus, Captain Pennington, Brother Jean, and Eliza Fisk seated in a semicircle. They were having a party to celebrate Captain Pennington's forthcoming marriage to Mrs. Fisk! Brother Nessus had just finished playing a tune on his violoncello and was sipping his wine. Then Captain Pennington said he was going to recite a poem, a verse of his own making, in honour of his new fiancée.

No! His poetry was worse than pig swill and almost made my eyes water. Brother Nessus seemed tickled by the news, however. He took another sip of wine and clapped his chubby, hoof-like hands. In his full dress reds, Captain Pennington stood at attention, then pulled a piece of paper from his pocket, cleared his throat twice, and began to read:

"With Passion my heart is laden.
Eliza, my dewy-lipped Maiden!
My Deliverance, my Sweet!
I hasten to thee on winged feet!

Not Zeus in all his Glory,
Could envision this Betrothal Story!
Anon, the Clarion of War Calls Me,
A Kindred Spirit of My Misery.

Hark! With Trembling Bosom she calls my name
Hard by yon Stream! O Sword and Fame!
I fight, I bleed, I fight the Enemy!
A soldier to Thy wayful Fancy!"

You would have thought Pennington had just read from Homer's *Odyssey* the way everyone carried on so, especially Brother Nessus. I thought he was going to crawl over on his hands and knees and start licking Captain Pennington's boots. As for me, I felt as if I were going to gag. When I glanced over at White Dog, he was laughing so hard the tears were falling from his eyes. Madeline, though, looked pale as a sheet. I think it finally hit her that life with Captain Pennington and Mrs. Fisk might not be all she had hoped it would be. I surely felt sorry for her.

We lay down again by the fire — me, Madeline, and White Dog — closer than ever, but in very different moods. The pine logs threw off bursts of sparks and reminded me of the night before when the Redcoats were shooting their arrows and Franklin's balloon had fallen from the sky. Only the night before! So much had happened since then, and my life had changed in so many ways. As I was thinking these thoughts, Mrs. Fisk walked into the room. She had pale yellow hair done up in a bun and was wearing a long wool dress. Madeline jumped up and ran into her arms.

"Mother!" she signed.

"Aren't you going to introduce me to your friends?" Mrs. Fisk asked.

I was introduced first. Mrs. Fisk apologized to me because she had not yet learned all the home signs. But I understood her perfectly when she signed to me that she would be taking the midday meal here with Madeline. When Madeline introduced White Dog, he commenced to sniff Mrs. Fisk's sleeve. She drew away her hand, more in surprise than anything else.

"Do not worry, Mother," Madeline signed. "He won't hurt you."

Suddenly, Brother Nessus charged forward from his place at the door, where he had been watching us, and struck White Dog with his cane. "Stop!" he shouted. "You are not an animal!" He turned to Mrs. Fisk. "I apologize, madam."

You could see that Mrs. Fisk was upset. She took Madeline's hand and led her from the room. Brother Nessus looked as if he had swallowed a hornet. White Dog glared at him and growled.

"I saw strange tracks leading to the barn," Brother Nessus said. "It looked as if *something* had recently been dragged across the snow. What have you boys been up to?"

"Nothing," I signed, putting the most innocent expression on my face that I could muster.

"Do not make those blasphemous figures in the air," he ordered. "Speak! Speak words the way I have taught you! There is nothing wrong with you. You are lazy, that's all! Lazy! Now tell me, what have you been up to?"

With my hands I repeated, "Nothing."

To punish me for impertinence, Brother Nessus made me walk around the orphanage one hundred times with a heavy pine log on my shoulders. This favourite punishment of his was called "Circumnavigating the Globe." As I carried the heavy, wet log on my shoulders, I wished Brother Nessus would take a swim in River No River with the log attached to his head like a hat.

It began to snow. I was sweating like a pig by the ninety-ninth turn, but when I glanced up, I saw Madeline and White Dog watching me from a window in the orphanage.

CHAPTER IX

Brother Nessus Smells a Rat

At the midday meal I sat at the head table next to Brother Jean and White Dog. Dr. Franklin was there, too, with Madeline and Mrs. Fisk. White Dog insisted on eating from a bowl without using a fork or spoon — the old-fashioned way, just bending his face down into the food.

We were having beans baked in maple sugar and bear grease, my favourite. Captain Pennington, all puffed up from his poetry reading, had to return to the barracks and sent his apologies. Brother Jean said grace, then quickly introduced Franklin to everyone as Monsieur Saunders, a travelling printer in need of work.

Brother Nessus arrived late. He had been drinking at Captain Pennington's party and was unsteady on his feet. He saw Franklin and smelled a rat. The moment he set eyes on the inventor I could tell he was suspicious. Brother Nessus sat down and refilled his glass with red wine.

Franklin inquired as to what the girls at the orphanage did in the way of schoolwork. He recommended the girls learn Latin, Greek, astronomy, and mathematics. "Women should learn the same things as men," he concluded. "This would put them in good stead to make their livings independently and not on the whims of a husband." He had realized this fact, he said, ever since one of his printers died and the widow, a Dutchwoman, had kept the books, managed the business, *and* raised a family.

Out of the corner of my eye I saw Madeline smile.

"I could not agree more, Mr. Saunders," Mrs. Fisk said. "You do know I print a little publication every month called *The King's News*, don't you? It's a broadside containing entertainment of interest to Loyalist readers. I might just have some work for you. I have been having some trouble with the press. It jams during the print run which, as you know, is most annoying, and costly besides. Would you have time to inspect the press and give me an estimate some time as to the repair?" She handed him a small piece of paper across the table. "Here is my address. I expect to speak with you soon."

"Indeed, ma'am," Franklin said. "I will be in touch with you. Feel free to contact me at your convenience."

What did Franklin think he was doing? I wondered.

Brother Nessus looked on with a sour face. "Sir," he said sneeringly, "you seem to pick at your food. Are you worried about something? Is it that the Rebels were driven back last night by our loyal troops?"

"It is a habit of mine to eat little at the midday but well at breakfast," Franklin replied. "But this was not always so. When I was a young printer in Boston, I took it in my head to live on bread and water. This regimen, notwithstanding the labour of being a printer, continued for six weeks. I ate a pound of bread a day and drank aught but water yet perceived no weakness in my body or mind and no loss of vigour."

"So!" Brother Nessus exclaimed. "You are an American!"

"I lived in England for many years. My tastes are international."

Brother Nessus took a sip of wine and ended up with a drop quivering on the end of his purple nose. I had to look away to stop myself from laughing. Once, a long time ago, I asked Brother Nessus if I could place my hand on the shiny wood of his violoncello while he played so I could feel the vibrations. I used to love the feel of music through my fingers. Brother Nessus only scowled, pursed his lips, and shook his head. He told me he did not want anyone to touch the instrument because it was too valuable. Later I learned that he gave music lessons and allowed his favourite students, his *pets*, as he called them, to play his violoncello whenever they pleased.

Brother Nessus didn't like me because I was Deaf and thought I was somehow less a person than the hearing students. He also did not like that I loved to fish. Brother Nessus thought it was a pastime for the lazy and did not understand fishing. He did not appreciate how mystical it was and would get angry because I cleaned the fish I caught but would not wash my hands afterwards. The Brother said I stank like fish, but I found it was a sweet, clean smell. It was the smell of rivers and wildness and the stars at night. I liked cutting the fish open with my knife, gutting them, and seeing if they were male or female. I always checked to see if there were fish eggs, "roe," because Cook and I loved eating roe fried in butter.

During the meal, I noticed that Brother Nessus was getting drunker by the minute. Whenever he drank too much it made us all nervous. Brother Jean seemed a bit pale. I guessed he would rather not have Brother Nessus interrogating Franklin any further. Madeline stirred her food listlessly with her spoon and did not look up.

Before Brother Nessus could ask Franklin more questions, I scribbled on a scrap of paper, "Tell us a story, Mr. Saunders!" and handed the message to the inventor.

Franklin peered at the piece of paper and smiled at me. "Michael asks me to tell a story."

All the other orphans at the table chimed in, "A story! Tell us a story," until Brother Jean quieted them.

Franklin took the hint. "Would you like to hear about the time I saved a man from drowning?"

All those at the table, except, of course, Brother Nessus, clapped their hands and urged him to continue.

Franklin cleared his throat and began. "When I was Michael's age, perhaps a little older, I lived in Boston and sought to find work at a printing house in New York. I sold some of my books to pay for passage on board a sloop bound for that city. I did not know anyone there and had very little money in my pocket. Once arrived, I offered my service to a printer but could find no employment. The proprietor told me of work to be had in Philadelphia, one hundred miles farther on. I left on a boat that day, so desperate was I for work." Here he paused for dramatic effect.

"When we were crossing the bay, a squall came up and tore the sail to pieces. One of the passengers was drunk —" everyone looked at Brother Nessus, who had suddenly discovered the bauble of wine on the end of his nose "— and fell overboard. To prevent him from drowning, I reached into the water, pulled him out by his hair, and dragged him back into the boat.

"At first he was angry to be so treated and cursed me up and down, but before he went to sleep, after he sobered a little and realized I had saved him from certain death, he gave me a gift. It was a copy of a book he had been carrying inside his coat when he fell into the water. It was soggy and needed a good drying out, but it proved to be my old favourite, *The Pilgrim's Progress*, written in Dutch and finely printed on good paper with copper cuts. The book was better bound than I had ever seen it in English. I have since found that it has been translated into most of the languages of Europe and suppose it has been more generally read than any other book, except perhaps the Bible."

Everyone applauded, except Brother Nessus, of course. He was watching White Dog, who had his face buried appreciatively in his food bowl, sucking up his dinner. Brother Nessus seemed so infuriated by what he saw as a lack of manners that he stood and struck White Dog across his back with his cane with such force that it broke in two. "That little savage eats like a pig," he slurred.

"Leave the boy alone," Franklin said. "What difference does it make as long as he eats?"

"It is not your business," Brother Nessus said. His face was flushed with drink.

"Sir," Franklin retorted, "a little wine is necessary to make some of us accomplished orators, but I fear in your case this is not true."

Brother Nessus laughed scornfully. "You will be interested to know that the woman who cooked your food is a former slave. Isn't it true that your George Washington owns slaves? And your Thomas Jefferson?"

"That may be true," Franklin said, staring directly into his eyes, "but human slavery is an abomination and I have written so."

Brother Nessus smirked. "Ah! You are a writer?"

I thought Brother Jean would burst, he looked so nervous.

"Of minor pamphlets, et cetera." Franklin knew he had said a bit too much. "A poor scribe is all I am."

I suspected that Brother Nessus would contact his friend, Captain Pennington, before the night was through to ferret out the real identity of this suspicious American printer, Richard Saunders.

We finished the meal in uncomfortable silence.

CHAPTER X

We Receive Bad News

Once upon a time the orphanage had produced its own little newspaper. The press had not been used in many years, however, and we were missing some of our "sorts," or the metal characters used in printing. The nearest foundry was across the ocean in London, England, at Palmer's Printing House, where Franklin had once worked. As we were leaving the dining room after the disastrous midday meal with Brother Nessus, Brother Jean turned to Franklin and asked if he would mind going downstairs to see if the printing press could be fixed. Madeline, White Dog, and I went with him. Mrs. Fisk stayed upstairs making last-minute arrangements with Brother Jean concerning Madeline's adoption.

In the basement, we combed through the compos- ing trays of old printer's type. White Dog rummaged around on his hands and knees and found some missing type under the press. All Madeline and I discovered were cobwebs, dust, and mice pellets. While he looked over the press, the inventor spoke to us about the nature of music and harmonics. He said the note of G was the sound of thunder, the sound of thunder was the colour red, and the colour red was the roll of a drum.

Franklin studied a few of the sorts we had left. He wrote down which letters were missing. While he worked, he talked about how a word may be spelled several different ways and, according to a theory of his, using fewer letters. He told us he had concluded that six letters of the alphabet, *c, j, q, w, x,* and *y,* weren't really needed. He proposed to replace these six letters with six new letters of his own devising.

"The only problem," he said, "is that every printer's type would have to be changed. And how on earth would you get everyone to agree to learn a new alphabet?" We were all laughing when Brother Jean came downstairs with the dreadful news.

A dry-goods merchant in town had been arrested that morning with an incriminating letter from none other than Benjamin Franklin. It was all over town — Franklin must be somewhere in Quebec City. The merchant was jailed, Brother Jean said, and would surely be charged with treason. The letter apparently contained information crucial to the American cause.

"Captain Pennington just came by with the news," Brother Jean said, sitting on a nearby stool and running his fingers through his white hair. "The British have posted guards along the shores of the St. Lawrence and on the roads and exits out of Quebec City. They have vowed to capture Franklin at any cost."

Brother Jean told Madeline that Mrs. Fisk had rushed home to print a special issue of her pamphlet about the hunt for Ben Franklin. Before leaving with Captain Pennington, Madeline's new mother had smiled and whispered to Brother Jean that she "smelled a hanging." She would be back on Friday to collect Madeline and her belongings.

The great Franklin sat deep in thought. What were we going to do?

CHAPTER XI

The Dictionary and Lexicon of Home Signs

Brother Jean went back upstairs. The rest of us sat silently by the old printing press. I felt at that moment that I would die on the gallows for sure.

"They must have used the restoring fluid," Franklin said, pacing across the room. "I have got to somehow get that letter through to General Washington."

"How?" I signed. "There are soldiers everywhere looking for you. They will be watching for letters … anything." White Dog translated my signing for Franklin.

"I must get the letter through. People's lives are at stake."

We needed a new secret code. Sympathetic stain was no longer an option. All of us paced the basement, wracking our brains to come up with a solution. We raced through possibilities but nothing seemed right.

"What about another type of invisible ink?" Madeline signed, and White Dog translated for Franklin's benefit.

"Well, vinegar has been used as ink," Franklin said. "The letter is blank until you hold it over the flame of a candle and the words reappear."

"Does this method work?" I signed.

"Sometimes, but I worry that now that the British know I am here they will be looking for any correspondence. Any paper they find will look suspicious. They would surely test a blank paper over a flame. It is a well-known subterfuge."

The four of us sat and thought some more.

"There is a cipher code where letters, symbols, or numbers are used in place of real words," Franklin said. "To decode a cipher, the person who gets the letter must have a key to know what the coded letters, symbols, or words really mean. I sometimes use the Bible for cipher codes. Spies often use commonplace books like Blackstone's *Commentaries on the Laws of England* or a standard dictionary. Unfortunately, these codes can be deciphered."

Franklin needed something different. Something that would really confound the British. If this letter didn't get through, he said, there would be tremendous loss of life. The minutes passed. Every so often we would look at one another and shake our heads. I think we all felt death's chariot hurrying near. Madeline jumped up.

"What is it?" Franklin asked.

Madeline tried to explain what she wanted to say, but she was too excited. She took a piece of paper and a pen from the sideboard and began writing words and drawing pictures. "We could use our home signs as a code," she wrote. "Home-signing symbols could be drawn as figures on paper. Since the symbols and their meanings would be known only to the people who used them, it would be foolproof."

"A brilliant idea!" Franklin said.

It was. Truly brilliant.

"But there is one catch," Franklin said. "How do we let General Washington know what the symbols mean? Most people don't understand your home signs. I certainly do not, at least not yet. It is like another language. Your sign for *moon* might be interpreted as *tree*. The sign for *tree* might be read as the sign for *fish*."

"Somehow the sender and receiver must have a chart with the symbols and their corresponding meanings," I wrote.

Madeline sat back down. Minutes passed. One of us would get an idea, start to explain it, then realize it wouldn't work. Franklin wondered if a chart could be made of home-signing symbols. But what kind of chart? It could not look like a secret code or draw attention to itself. So what could it be?

"I know," Madeline wrote. "We shall write the code like a dictionary. We can call it *The Dictionary and Lexicon of Home Signs*. It would have illustrations. The home signs would be drawn with their corresponding meanings."

"Of course," Franklin said. "We will make each copy look like a dictionary and bind them like books. We will make it look as much like a standard dictionary as possible. The person who delivers the dictionary to my contact will carry a note that he is delivering a charitable dictionary to a fictitious asylum for the Deaf."

"I will deliver the dictionary, Mr. Franklin," I signed. "No one will suspect me, because I am Deaf. They will just dismiss me like everyone does."

Franklin shook my hand and told me my bravery would not go unrewarded. He then went upstairs to speak with Brother Jean, leaving us to our monumental task.

Madeline, White Dog, and I began preparing some of the signs for the cipher book. Madeline illustrated the signs for *British*, *storm*, *river*, *come*, *go*, *secret*, *spy*, *ladder*, *difficulty*, *soldiers*, *paper*, *camp*, *Redcoats*, and the rest of the words that Franklin had outlined, including the alphabet and numbers up to one hundred. She interspersed these vital signs with everyday symbols for words like *dog* and *cat* to make the book seem like a proper dictionary.

When the day darkened, White Dog went out hunting. Madeline and I sat up together, a lone candle to light our pages, and listed the whole of our home-signing language. We became immersed in the whole project. I think we probably overdid it, because we ended up with a dictionary that contained about ten times as much information as what was needed. It just felt good to make our language legitimate. No one paid attention to the Deaf unless it was to lock them away. That was why home-signing made for a great spy code. Franklin needed an invisible language, and we, the Deaf, were an invisible people — abandoned, chained up in asylums, denied the right to communicate. In a way, we were perfect spies.

In the morning, after a hurried breakfast, Franklin, Madeline, and I returned to the press to begin the printing and book-binding. Making a book was like making a fishing fly. You needed a good eye, good hands, and patience. We realized we had to make more than a single dictionary. We needed a copy for Franklin and his spy contact, plus two other copies in case those got lost.

Franklin said he used to lay out and print a newspaper in a few hours, so he figured we might be able to finish the job in a couple of days. Printing the dictionary was going to be the easy part. We had Madeline's sketches:

drawings of hands, the different shapes they took, and their meanings. Woodblock carving would take too much time, so we etched the drawings onto copperplate.

We could not have got the whole project done without Brother Jean's help. He kept Brother Nessus out of our way and let us sneak down to the printing press in the basement when we were supposed to be in bed. I was the proofreader, and I was proud to say we did not make any typographical errors. I was glad, because if there had been a mistake we would have had to reset the type of each offending page.

The finishing touch was the binding. We all helped fold the pages under Franklin's gaze. Fold once, you got two leaves or four pages — a folio. Fold again, you got four leaves or eight pages — a quarto. Our book was a quarto.

It was important to make the creases in the paper flat, so we creased them with a flat cow-bone folder that Franklin had in the collection of instruments he carried around in his pockets. Madeline sewed the pages together with linen thread. We wanted the dictionary to be sturdy, so we laced cords, onto which the pages had been sewn, through holes in thin wood cover boards. Then we left the books overnight between two pine planks, weighed down with an anvil. This pressed out the swelling in the paper.

The books started to look like books! We covered them with pigskin with glue made from wheat flour and water that Cook made in the kitchen. We did not have time to stamp the lettering on the covers with gold leaf, which was the fancy way, so instead we pasted paper labels printed with the title on the cover of each book.

Each book was seven inches tall, five inches wide, and had over one hundred pages.

They were beautiful books. Tomorrow I would take one to Franklin's contact, a farmer named Johnson who lived near Quebec City.

Madeline and I were overwhelmed with our effort. The illustrations were beautiful. Each was a perfect representation of the signs that were our only lifeline to the world if only the world were sympathetic enough to listen. Franklin and White Dog knew that making this book had become important to Madeline and me. It was not just finishing the dictionary; we knew we would miss each other. But Madeline was happy. She was getting a new family, a second chance. That was all that mattered. As for me, I only hoped to stay alive.

CHAPTER XII

Dr. Franklin Electrifies a Turkey to the Amazement of All

The next morning Madeline left the orphanage for good. Brother Jean had tears in his eyes, even though she was only moving across town. When she said goodbye, she removed her red scarf and gave it to me.

"I don't know what you can use it for, Michael," she signed. "Maybe you can use the threads to make a pretty fly." Then she kissed me on both cheeks and climbed into the waiting sleigh with Mrs. Fisk. Captain Pennington was driving.

It could have been my imagination, but Pennington seemed to stare at Franklin before Mrs. Fisk prompted him to drive on. Madeline turned and gave us a smile and a wave. I watched the sled disappear into the woods.

"Cheer up," Franklin said. "The dictionary is done. Think of it as a product of your friendship with Madeline. You will always have Madeline because you will always have the accomplishment of the dictionary."

He was right. How could I be sad when we had achieved so much? Now the spy letters would get through to their destinations. Now perhaps Franklin would be safe.

After we saw Madeline off, we walked back to the orphanage. We noticed Brother Nessus standing drunkenly by the turkey pen, speechifying to a group of orphans. He said he was going to kill a turkey for dinner. Killing the birds was White Dog's job. Brother Nessus did not know how to do it without making the animals suffer terribly. White Dog stood by the turkey pen and growled at Brother Nessus.

"Brother Nessus, how do you propose to dispatch such a large bird?" Franklin asked. "With your cane? If you club it to death, the meat will not be tasty."

"I will swing it around by its neck until its body flies off," Brother Nessus said sourly. This time it appeared the Brother had really gone mad!

"Wouldn't it be more humane to electrify the bird?" Franklin proposed.

Everyone stopped immediately and listened. Brother Nessus would have none of it and said it was preposterous. But Franklin said he proposed to kill the turkey with an electric charge from a Leyden jar.

What was he doing? He would give himself away! The only Leyden jars were attached to the basket of the balloon. We were trying to keep Franklin's identity a secret, especially from Brother Nessus. What was the inventor thinking? I saw us swinging from the gallows and imagined the funeral orations, what Madeline would say.

"Michael," Franklin said, pulling me from my reverie and speaking to me in a low voice so no one else could hear, "show me to the *Liberty*. I believe I have some Leyden jars stowed around the basket."

Franklin could now understand most of my home signs. As I led him to the barn where we had hidden the airship. I tried to reason with him. "If Brother Nessus does not already know you are Ben Franklin, he surely will if you bring out one of your wonderful bottles."

But it was no use. The scientist was determined. He climbed inside the airship and threw things out onto the straw: a clock, a weathervane, a lightning rod, a small case that rattled when it hit the ground, a glass globe, and a quantity of provisions, namely, a bag of sugar, a pound of tea, two pounds of ground coffee, a small cask of Madeira wine, a block of Gloucester cheese, biscuits, and three pounds of raisins. The food he instructed to be taken into the orphanage for the enjoyment of all the boys and girls. He talked a little about the ship, and I could tell he wanted to take it into the air again. Franklin fumbled about with some copper wires and a box with a crank, and it wasn't long before he had powered up half a dozen of the jars, which glowed brightly.

The inventor picked up two of these glowing jars and walked casually into the turkey pen where the birds clucked and strutted about like harmless fools. Brother Nessus sneered. Franklin was about to prod one of the turkeys when the jars discharged into his body with a loud crack. He fell backwards and did not get up.

The great Franklin is dead, I thought. *And it is all my fault.* When I looked at Brother Nessus, he was laughing.

By and by, however, the scientist stood up, collected his thoughts, charged two other Leyden jars, and shocked one of the birds, which died immediately. All agreed after dinner, except for Brother Nessus, of course, that the meat was uncommonly tender.

CHAPTER XIII

I Become a Spy

T he next morning I got up before the Sun and went out to do my milking. But I did not go to the cow barn. I had bribed one of the other boys to do my milking for me by promising him one of the spent Leyden jars and my portions of dinner meat for the next week. I had *The Dictionary and Lexicon of Home Signs* hidden inside my jacket. It was wrapped in brown paper with a fictitious address — the Asylum for Experiments in the Communication of Deaf Inmates.

I put the book in a cloth bag and slung it over my shoulder. Skirting around the cow barn, I headed through the woods. I had some trouble poling the raft across the river as the water was high from the runoff, but I finally made it to the other side. I knew I could be a spy and that I would not be too scared.

As I walked down the road towards the farm owned by Franklin's operative, I could see the British sentry post in the distance and two Redcoat soldiers. I braced myself. *I am Michael Flynn and I am not afraid of anything.*

One of the Redcoats was tall and skinny and without a hat. He had red hair and his face had red spots on it. The other one was also tall, but he had black hair and a large mole on his narrow chin. They both appeared to be about eighteen.

"Halt!" the spotted one shouted.

I knew I had to act calm, but my heart was pounding.

"What's in that bag, boy?" the other soldier demanded.

"A dictionary, sir," I signed.

He laughed. "The boy's a loon!"

"Ask again, Roger," the red-haired soldier said.

"What's in that bag, boy?"

Again I signed, and again the young men doubled over with laughter. The red-haired one with the spots grabbed the bag from me, removed the book, and was about to rip off the paper when the other sentry stopped him.

"Wait," he said. "What's the address?"

"Some kind of Asylum for the Deaf."

"An Asylum for the Deaf?" the dark-haired one echoed, confused.

While they talked, I took out the note I had brought that explained the book was a dictionary for Deaf people and that the Asylum for Experiments in the Communication of Deaf Inmates was a special school.

When I showed the dark-haired Redcoat the paper, he read it, then crumpled it up and threw it on the ground. "I never 'eard of no such school. You ever 'eard of this school, Jack?"

"I never heard of it neither, Roger." The spotted one peered at me. "You Canadians are a queer lot, ain't you? Look at your vest. What are those things?"

"Flies, sir," I wrote.

"Flies! Haw-haw!"

"It's a trick," the dark-haired one said. "The boy's trying to get our attention away from the book."

"It might explode," the other one said.

"No, stupid, it won't explode. It's a book."

The spotted sentry ripped off the brown paper and read through the dictionary. My heart sank. "What's all this funny stuff?" he demanded. "Looks suspicious to me."

"No, look, I will show you," I wrote. And I showed him how I could sign with my hands.

"That's queer, ain't it?" the dark-haired soldier said.

The spotted one nodded. "I seen some Indians do that once. Talked to each other with their hands. It was a right strange sight." He seemed to have convinced himself, but then he grabbed me by the shirt and gave me a shake.

"Ah, let 'im go," the dark-haired Redcoat said. "What 'arm could a loon be?"

"You're right. He's just an idiot boy."

I put the book back into my bag, and they let me through the checkpoint. I had to stop myself from breaking into a run as the sweat poured off me.

When I got to the farm, I saw the wooden box that usually held the salt lick for the cows. That was where Franklin had told me to leave the book. I glanced around. There was no one in sight. I opened the box and slid the book in. Then I pulled some red threads from the shawl Madeline had given me and tied them to the branch of a nearby tree as a signal. Madeline would have been proud of me. I turned to make my way back to the orphanage. My job was done.

CHAPTER XIV

Poor Mrs. Fisk

That night, around midnight, I woke with a start. Something was wrong. I got out of bed and went to the window. I don't know what I thought I would see.

It was Madeline. She waved up at me to come outside. She had ridden one of her new mother's horses over and had tied the reins to a tree. I ran downstairs. When I got to her, I could see she was crying. I had never seen her so upset. She signed that her new mother had been arrested and that the Redcoats were on their way to the orphanage to capture Franklin.

"But your mother is a Loyalist. She's British —"

"Oh, Michael!" Madeline cried. "She is not British. She is a spy. A spy like Franklin!"

And then I understood the quick exchange of the paper at the dinner table. Mrs. Fisk was one of Franklin's contacts! I grabbed Madeline's hand, and we ran into the orphanage and up the stairs towards Franklin's room.

In my mind, I cried out, *Run! They are coming! They are after you! Run!*

We rounded the corner and burst into Franklin's bedroom.

He was gone!

CHAPTER XV

We Prepare for the Worst

It was the hour of the wolf. I did not want to wake Brother Jean, because the noise might rouse Brother Nessus, who slept in the next room. I took Madeline's hand, and together we walked to the ladder that led to Cook's attic room. I had been afraid of the secrets inside that room ever since my visit there with White Dog. Cook had strong spirits around her, but I loved her.

There was no reason to be afraid, I told myself. The British were on their way, and Cook was our only hope. I climbed the ladder first. When I pushed up the trap-door, I smelled beeswax and cinnamon.

Out of the blackness Cook's face appeared. "Michael? Is that you? What is the matter, child?"

I almost didn't recognize her. She was wearing a night hat and a long nightgown. No flowing robes or ceremonial makeup. She looked normal. Just like Cook. I breathed a sigh of relief and tumbled into her arms. Madeline pulled herself up the ladder and into the room behind me.

"Madeline!" Cook cried. "What on earth are you doing here! Your mother will be worried sick!"

Cook made us sit with her on the floor. She lit three large candles and would not let me sign and explain the situation until the last candle was ignited. "Now, Michael, please tell me what is going on."

I poured everything out in signs to make her understand the danger we were in. "Madeline's new mother is not a Loyalist at all. She is an American spy who was working with Franklin all along. The British came and arrested her tonight …"

Madeline nodded.

"And now," I continued, "the Redcoats are on their way here to arrest Franklin. We went to his room to warn him and —"

"He was gone?" Cook finished my sentence.

"Yes!" Madeline signed frantically. "How did you know?"

Cook rose and took a scroll from a small wooden chest on the windowsill. "I was supposed to give you this when you got up this morning." She handed the scroll to me.

I unfurled the paper, but it was blank. "Cook, may I borrow one of your candles?"

She looked uncertain, but then brought a candle over for me. I held the paper above the flame. Just as I expected, a code began to appear. Signs and symbols — the signs and symbols we had used in the dictionary — wriggled like magic across the page.

Cook laughed. "Well, I never."

This is what the scroll said: "Danger — British know who I am — I swim upriver — White Dog — Cave — Madeline in danger — Redcoats take Mrs. Fisk — Will pray you safe — Wind blow you here I trust."

A stroke of genius! Franklin knew the Redcoats would never look for a man swimming upriver. He loved to swim. Most folks thought it unhealthy. I held the corner of the scroll over the candle flame, and we watched it turn to ash.

Madeline and I both kissed Cook, who pleaded with us to be careful, then we scooted down the ladder and out the door. The Sun was rising above the horizon. There were still patches of snow on the ground. It was one of those days when you could smell the Earth thawing.

When we arrived at River No River, I found a birch-bark canoe pulled up into the bush nearby. This was the canoe the Brothers kept for carrying provisions. I had ridden in it before but never without Brother Jean. The canoe was old and had been re-pitched with sap and re-sewn with the roots of a tamarack. Before we could launch the canoe, I spotted some Redcoats riding up to the door of the orphanage. They did not see us — we were too far away and under the shelter of a willow tree. I looked over at Madeline. Her face was wet with tears. I felt bad that she had found a mother and now had lost her. I would have done anything for Madeline.

"Wait here," I signed.

"No, Michael. It's not safe," Madeline signed back.

"Stay by the canoe. If I am not back soon, you go ahead to White Dog's cave without me."

"No, Michael! I won't leave you."

"I want Pennington to see me," I signed. "I don't want him to know I have left. If he thinks I don't know anything, he might divide his soldiers and send them searching all over the city. It will be easier for us to defeat them that way."

"I am not leaving you behind." Madeline may have understood and approved my plan, but she was not budging.

I smiled at her and signed, "You *are* stubborn."

CHAPTER XVI

*Captain Pennington Recites
More of His Awful Poetry*

I ran up to the orphanage and saw Captain Pennington. He was talking to Brother Nessus. Then they saw me, too.

"Where is he, boy?" Brother Nessus demanded, grabbing me. "Where is Benjamin Franklin?"

I shrugged and tried to look innocent.

"Liar!" Brother Nessus cried, raising his cane to strike me.

"No!" Brother Jean appeared at my side. "Leave him alone."

"You could be hanged for withholding the King's information," Pennington said to me. "You know who we mean. Glasses, bald head, unpowdered hair, a supercilious grin."

"We will search the traitor's room," Brother Nessus declared. "They have guards posted on all land routes. It is impossible for Franklin to escape."

"Shall we arrest the boy?" a soldier asked.

"You can't do that," Brother Jean cried. "He is under the protection of the orphanage."

"Let him go," the captain said. "He is a harmless fool. An idiot. He can't even speak. He just stands around and waves his arms." He gave an evil little grin. "Ah, that reminds me of a new poem I wrote. Would you men like to hear it?"

The men did not look as if they wanted to hear a poem. Captain Pennington cleared his throat and began to torture the English language the way a cruel child might pull the wings off a fly.

"When Danger is near,
And the Birds you can't hear
Remember who You are
British Men of War
Great Britain is great
We don't suffer Fools
Or stupid Imbeciles
It's the Cat-'o-Nine-Tails
To whomever We hate
Remember, Men, We fight
For Glory, for —"

"Oh, shut up!"

"Who said that?" Pennington looked around frantically.

No one spoke. Brother Jean laughed. But none of the soldiers owned up to the impertinence, so Pennington got back on his black horse.

"Now," he said, "back to business. A promotion to the man who helps me find Franklin. Alive. We will hang him and make a spectacle of his death."

The soldiers roared their approval.

Captain Pennington looked straight at me. "This boy here knows of a hideout upriver. I am told it belongs to the wild child." He smirked. "We will try there. Be careful, though. The wild boy has been known to fight like a savage."

"Go to your room," Brother Nessus said to me.

Brother Jean nodded at me to go.

"But I —"

"To your room," Brother Jean said.

I did as I was told. In my room, I took my beautiful fishing rod, tied a rope around it, and slung it over my shoulder like a gun. It was too lovely to leave behind. I tied some blankets together and, making sure they were secure, shinnied down the outside wall, making my escape.

But when I reached the ground, Pennington was waiting for me, pointing a musket at my chest.

"Put up your hands," he said.

Then, quick as magic, Cook appeared. She placed herself between Pennington and me and folded her arms.

"Out of the way, old woman," Pennington said.

"I'm not moving," she said. "Michael, don't be afraid. Go on down to the river."

"I'll shoot," Pennington said. "You and the boy."

"No, you won't," Cook said, grabbing the musket from his hands.

"Godspeed, Michael," she said, and I didn't need to lip-read another word.

When I got to the river, Madeline was waiting by the canoe.

"Hurry," I signed. "We must warn Franklin."

We pushed off in the canoe and began to paddle. We had to beat Pennington to White Dog's cave.

CHAPTER XVII

I Am Overcome by Guilt

The trip to White Dog's cave took two days. On the first day out I became overconfident. I reckoned Pennington's men were not sure of the exact location of the hideout, so I figured we had some time. Maybe it was because we were hungry and tired of eating roots. While we were paddling the canoe, I peered down through the clear water and thought I saw the big old trout that lived in one of the deepest pools of River No River.

What is he doing up here? I wondered. I had snagged him once, almost pulling him out of the water, but he got free. He was the granddaddy of all trout, but he was too wily, and I never did catch him. I saw him now and then, a shadow at the bottom of the pool. In the evening, he would float to the surface and swallow the flies that landed on the water. I had even seen him eat frogs when they were swimming across the river. White Dog said once he had seen the old trout eat the last mallard duckling in a single file of ducklings. That trout would eat anything. When I fished for him, I used any old bait, as long as it moved or was shiny.

Madeline and I stopped every so often and fished from the canoe. Once we pulled the canoe up onto a bank, hid the boat in the bush, and fished from the shore by a stand of mulberry and willow trees. I used one of my best flies. We took turns using my fly rod, but mostly I let Madeline use it. She knew how to cast downwind with the Sun just right so as not to cast a shadow and scare the trout. She threw the line out again and again so that the fly had little time to sink and as little as possible of the line was drowned. If a bluegill or trout saw the drowned line, he would not bite. She was a good angler, but she was not having any luck.

I had already caught a small trout. I watched Madeline cast her line. She was using an artificial fly of her own making — a pretty design with a body made of bear's hair wrapped in coloured silk and hackled with the gaudy feathers of a partridge. Madeline was a born angler, just like me, but she would not use live bait because she did not like putting the hook through a living thing.

Finally, she caught a nice trout. It flew out of the water and fought with her, but she reeled it in. The trout was a beauty. Madeline said we should head to White Dog's cave so we could arrive there before nightfall.

"What for?" I signed. "I think the granddaddy trout is about to strike. You are just mad that I am going to catch him and not you." I wanted to catch a big fish of my own to beat the one she had caught. I could be very competitive.

"Michael Flynn, you are the most difficult person in the whole world!"

97

So I tried and tried to catch the trout. One hour went by, then two. But I did not catch the fish. All I did was waste precious time.

That night I made a fire with flint and some dry yarn I carried in my pocket as a starter. The fire was small on account of I did not want to let the enemy know where we were. We cooked the trout on a spit over a fire and peeled the sweet flesh back with our hands. In the moonlight, I could see the fish jumping. Tormenting me.

Madeline and I said good-night. I saw her ask for her mother's safety in her home-signed prayers. Then she fell asleep.

I stayed awake for a while, counting the stars. I figured if the British found White Dog's cave, they would have to be careful. The cave was part of the spirit world. White Dog believed everything possessed an immortal soul. Even the rocks were alive. The spirits that protected White Dog's cave could be friendly, but if you had bad intentions, they could hurt or kill you. I wondered if Franklin was just a spirit of the sky who had fallen to Earth. I pictured the inventor falling from the sky, then I fell asleep.

In the morning, Madeline and I paddled upriver to the cave. We arrived there late in the morning and beached the canoe. You could not see the cave from the water, but I knew it was there, hidden among the firs in an alder grove at the top of the hill. Madeline and I were halfway up the hill, climbing through the thick underbrush — bunchberry, heather, and starflowers — when I saw the branches of the big willow tree at the cave mouth move. It was White Dog. He was making quick movements with his hands far away from his body. It was one of our home signs. He made the sign again.

Stay away.

He put his arm over his head in a horizontal position.

Danger.

On the opposite side of the hill I saw them, their red coats clearly visible against the trees. They had found the cave. It was an ambush. White Dog was trying to warn us.

Then everything happened at once. Franklin burst out of the cave and ran down the hill, headed right for us. The British moved after him at the same time, and I saw Pennington shout, "Take him alive!" But one of the soldiers fired, anyway, and a musket ball flew past Franklin's head, scattering the leaves of a tree. Another musket ball flew over my head with an awful vibration. Now two Redcoats were after Franklin. They threw down their muskets and were racing to catch him. White Dog came out of nowhere. He crashed into the soldiers like a wild animal and sent them sprawling. The soldiers were no match for White Dog's ferocity. Without their guns, they were helpless.

When Franklin finally reached us, he was all out of breath and wheezing. Madeline led him down to the canoe and helped him in. I signed to Madeline to hurry and push off from the shore. I wanted to make sure White Dog had not been injured, so I ran back up the hill to the cave, but he was gone. Birds flew above me as if nothing had happened, as if our war games amounted to nothing. All the world was still.

Returning to the shore, I saw Madeline and Franklin paddling downriver. She waved to me. I dived into the water and swam out to the canoe. Madeline helped to pull me in. I almost tipped us, but we managed to stay upright. Franklin asked me where White Dog was. I assured him that White Dog had probably run into the forest and would most likely meet us back at the orphanage.

We reached the orphanage on the second night. That was when we heard the news.

Brother Jean told us that Captain Pennington had arrested White Dog and thrown him into the Civil Asylum for Incorrigibles in Lower Town. He had been classified as a lunatic on account of the pictures on his skull and his nocturnal behaviour. He had also been designated an enemy of the King.

It was all my fault that White Dog was caught. If I had not lingered to fish, he would still be free. I took my beautiful fishing rod outside and snapped it in half. I vowed never to fish again.

CHAPTER XVIII

We Attempt to Rescue White Dog from the Civil Asylum for Incorrigibles

Madeline tried to stop me, but I had destroyed the fishing rod before she could reach me.

"Michael!" She shook me by the shoulders. "We must help White Dog. It wasn't just your fault. We both stopped to fish. We were wrong."

The only thing to do now was rescue him. We had to move fast. I took a leather strap and used it to secure my Mohawk knife to my forearm. I figured I might need it for more than just sharpening my writing quill. I motioned for Madeline to follow me, and we went to find Franklin.

The scientist was at the stables trying to drag his airship outside. He knew already that we would be going to rescue White Dog. Franklin had found a basket that had been used to transport cotton and had turned it into a makeshift passenger carrier to replace the airship's ruined one. The girls in the orphanage, under Madeline's direction, had repaired the fabric balloon. Franklin attached it to the basket and prepared it for flight with hot air from a small bonfire. Most of the

Leyden jars were broken, but he managed to charge and attach a few around the basket. He greased the sliding valves and roller bearings on the propeller. The rudder was barely working. Last of all, he found a long rope and threw it into the ship.

Franklin placed on board a bag of raisins, some maple sugar from Cook, a vial of water, a block of cheese, dried apples, a beef pie, and a mince pie. The provisions were for us — me, Madeline, and White Dog. The airship was ready to go. The chickens and turkeys stared at us forlornly from their pens. I expected they were relieved that Franklin did not pursue them with one of his electrical jars. Franklin and Madeline climbed into the basket. He motioned for me to untie the ropes. As soon as I did, the ship began to ascend. I managed to jump in just before the balloon was yanked into the sky.

The cold air felt good. From this height you could see the entire town. I noticed the Sun was setting and the Moon had already risen. We flew higher and higher, floating above the orphanage, the chicken coops, and the trees. We had a good wind and flew quickly. I could make out the Civil Asylum for Incorrigibles near the harbour where the River St. Charles emptied into the St. Lawrence. It was a grey building, two storeys high, with bars in the windows, surrounded by an enormous stone wall. I had no idea how many people were imprisoned there. And it was not just lunatics in that place. Brother Jean said there were people in there who had simply been living on the street — men, women, and children. And lots of Deaf people like Madeline and me.

We crossed over the wall, and as soon as we got close enough to hover over the building's courtyard, the inmates saw us. They were pressed against the bars of the windows in twos and threes. Their mouths were wide open, and I could tell they were screaming at the sight of the balloon. They waved their hands and pointed, some of them crying. Perhaps they cried because they thought it was the end of the world. The airship was certainly a spectacular sight. A girl, a boy, an old man with a telescope, and a flying machine. I thought, *Who is crazy? Them or us?*

We decided that Franklin would remain in the balloon and simply lower Madeline and me to the ground so we could make a quick getaway after we rescued White Dog. As soon as Franklin deposited us on the ground, we waved up to him and he manoeuvred the balloon off to the back of the building to wait. The rest was up to us.

Walking towards the front door, we passed a razor-thin woman in rags gathering stones. She did not even look at us. She was in her own world, counting pebbles. No one stopped us. We just strolled inside. I figured there were no locks because the guards didn't expect anyone to get over the wall. Brother Jean told me once that people paid money to tour the asylum and watch the antics of the crazy people.

Inside, the stench was awful. The asylum was so full of smoke from lamps and stoves that we could hardly see. Also, it was cold, bone-cold. Through the smoke I saw an old man. I wasn't sure if he was an inmate or a worker. He was tossing the pieces of a broken chair into a stove. Next to the stove was a pail of boiled mush. Ghostly figures stood waiting and trembling with bowls in their outstretched hands. After the old man stoked the fire with the broken chair, he began to ladle the mush into the bowls.

At the end of the line stood a boy. Madeline and I spotted him at the same time. White Dog! She ran over and took his arm, but when she wheeled him around it wasn't White Dog at all. The Deaf boy before us could not have been more than twelve or thirteen. His face was covered with scabs and bruises. I knew he was Deaf because he tried to communicate with me by signing something with his hands. He seemed to be begging me to do something, but I could not tell what exactly. I shuddered because it was like looking at myself.

The boy opened his mouth in a howl, and when he howled, the man who was serving food came over and hit him with the ladle so hard he knocked him down. From nowhere another man came, kicked the boy, and dragged him away into the darkness. We walked away slowly, afraid that sudden movements would call attention to us. I took Madeline's hand. We glanced behind us. Someone was closing and bolting the front door. We were trapped in the asylum!

Madeline and I continued to look for White Dog but could not find him. We came to the top of a damp stone stairway, descended the stairs, and entered a cavernous basement filled with cubicles. In each cubicle a man or woman was chained. Most of them did not wear clothes. They barely moved, but those who did had to strain against chains that bolted their wrists to the walls.

There were dogs everywhere. More dogs than people. They were skinny and mangy, and you could only see them on account of their eyes, which shone in the dark. People lay on straw and stared and rattled their chains at us as we passed. They were forced to lie in their own waste, and I reckoned they were never unchained. I remembered something Brother Jean had told me. He had said that mad people were not believed to feel heat, cold, or pain. The world thought that lunatics were not human.

Madeline and I had almost given up hope when we saw White Dog. He was crouched under a long wooden bench. A group of old people sat on the bench, howling and cursing or staring at the wall and whispering. White Dog was shackled to the bench with a chain around his wrist. He looked up when he noticed us and began to cry.

"You are here!" he gasped. "They caught you, too."

"No, we are here to rescue you," Madeline signed.

White Dog stared at us and attempted a smile. I used my knife to pick the lock on his chains. Madeline talked to White Dog while I worked. He was scared. She told him to think about the animals that were tattooed on his skull and how they would protect him. White Dog said they were animals that he had dreamed. A medicine man had tattooed the animals onto his skull. The medicine man had told him that dreams were important for people, especially for young men so that they could be strong, independent, and brave.

"The animals will protect you," Madeline signed.

Finally, I got the lock open and freed White Dog. We all ran up the stairs towards the back of the building where White Dog thought we would find a door to the outside. The manacle and part of the chain were still attached to White Dog's wrist. The back door of the asylum was locked with a deadbolt, but we found a small abandoned kitchen and crawled through a delivery hole to the outside. But there, waiting for us, was Captain Pennington and two of his soldiers. The captain aimed a flintlock pistol at us.

"Did you think you could get away that easily?" Pennington asked.

White Dog lashed out with his chain, striking the barrel. The pistol fired and wounded one of the soldiers. White Dog jumped onto the other soldier and sank his teeth into the man's arm. Madeline and I tried to overpower Pennington, but he was a tall, strong man and we could not take him down. So I took out my knife. When Pennington felt the blade against his neck, he stopped struggling. White Dog took their guns, and the three of us backed away. I held out my knife as protection.

The captain stared at me. He held his neck where my blade had nicked him. When he took his hand away, there was blood. "I will see you hang," he vowed.

Madeline nudged me in the ribs and pointed at the sky. Franklin's balloon was descending into the asylum courtyard. We ran for the balloon, but what I did not know was that Pennington had another pistol and was reloading it with propellant powder.

White Dog reached the basket first. He made a step by locking the fingers of both hands and hoisted Madeline into the basket. Then he helped me in. When I was safely in the basket, I reached out and grasped White Dog's hand. I was hauling him up when I felt the shot. Captain Pennington had shot White Dog in the back. My friend's eyes looked into mine for a moment, and then he let go of my hand and fell to the courtyard. The balloon rose higher and higher. White Dog's eyes were open. He lay dying, and I could do nothing for him. A flock of bats wheeled across the sky. We rose above the asylum where White Dog lay lifeless on the ground. Then up we went and we were gone.

CHAPTER XIX

The Brandywine

Madeline and I huddled in a corner of the basket as we sailed away from the asylum. I held her in my arms. She was crying. We flew due south. Franklin said our present course would take us to Vermont, then, if the winds were right, to New York.

After a few hours of flight, Franklin gave Madeline a present he had made just for her. It was a wooden music box. Inside the box was a disc that he had constructed from a copper barrel lid he had found in the stables. He had etched notes in the metal and had built a kind of crankcase. By turning the crank, one could, he said, produce a most beautiful sound. Aware that she could not hear the notes, he suggested that she first "read" the impressions with her fingers, then place her hand on the box and feel the vibrations of the music through the wood. Madeline played the box while we sailed and stopped crying. She would not communicate with either of us for a long time.

The balloon floated in the skies. We had to be careful, even in the dark. We did not want to be seen by soldiers, or farmers, or people on horseback, or anyone else. What would someone say if they saw an airship floating through the clouds at night, luminous across the crescent Moon? They would say they were crazy. Crazy and seeing things. And after that they would contact the Royal Dragoons. We did not want to take any chances.

Franklin said the airship hummed when it moved. He said the sound was like the wind on your face. The Moon was large and beautiful. Madeline wondered if by getting closer we could achieve a state of weightlessness. There was a telescope on board through which we observed the planets, especially Mars, which was bright red. With the telescope we could see the canals on Mars and what appeared to be oceans and craters on the Moon. It seemed to me that people must live on Mars and on the Moon, too. Franklin kept busy at his calculations. There was a meteor shower that streaked across the sky, leaving liquid trails of fire so close to the ship I thought I might touch them. We were in another world, one free from war, floating above everything.

While Franklin charted the stars and wrote notes, Madeline made drawings for his astrological projections. And there were the clouds. What clouds! They were solid, like a white wall, but we magically passed through them. We slipped through one wall of cloud, then another. The clouds left us damp and smelling like the sea. Then we could not see, and it was all pure white until we broke through the other side of the cloud into the indigo night sky. Madeline's hair was hanging wet around her face, and Franklin's was soaked.

Once I saw a battle raging beneath us and smoke from the muskets of the soldiers. I spied a horseman riding on an empty road. He galloped with such speed that he seemed to keep pace with the airship. I spotted a farmer ploughing a field, and a carriage racing down a dirt road, and pigs, and sheep, and cows, and boats navigating a canal.

Later, with the stars around us, a flock of Canada geese flew by, almost grazing the ship with the tips of their wings. Franklin told me that Christopher Columbus had kept a journal when he discovered America, and in one of his entries the explorer had written that the flocks of parrots were so thick they obscured the Sun.

We did not need to hear up here. It was silent, anyway. Franklin made notes about the wind. He concluded that the wind had no pattern and that its movements were dependent on the whims of the Sun and Moon. He had an idea that people could harness the wind. Maybe that would make ocean voyages faster. He also believed the oceans had regular currents that resembled underwater streams, or jets of water, and that we could make the oceans work for us, too. But he did not believe men could stop fighting long enough to do these things.

Franklin talked until dawn. It seemed that he did not need to sleep. He talked about space and time. He talked about the planets, and he talked about war. Franklin said his war was against Ignorance and Tyranny. He talked about being an old man. He said his time on Earth would end soon but ours was just beginning.

In the morning, when the sky was still dark, Venus and the crescent Moon pierced the twilight above the southeast horizon. Mars, the warrior planet, hovered at the same height above the southwest horizon. There was a strange feeling in the air. Franklin said the red planet had swung so close to Earth that it was actually closer than Venus.

"Look!" he said. "Look through the telescope!"

We could see polar icecaps on Mars and what appeared to be frozen cities. Was Mars the warrior planet? I was a warrior now. My enemy was the lowdown, boneless army of men who hurt the weak and defenceless.

Then came the lightning. Electricity swirled around us and my bones tingled. All the while, Franklin jotted down notes and peered anxiously at his instruments. I gazed at the compass. The needle was spinning around wildly. The balloon began to descend softly as if it were being pulled to the ground by some mysterious force.

I thought we would have a peaceful landing, but on the way down we hit a tree. The branches broke our fall, but the basket overturned and the ship caught fire from the stove that we carried on board. We were lucky to be alive. All we could do was watch the balloon burn. Everything was gone: Franklin's journal, the papers containing his star calculations, everything!

So we walked. We did not know where we were, but we eventually found ourselves on the outskirts of an abandoned village whose houses were overgrown with weeds. The barns had collapsed like old wooden skeletons. Out of nowhere an old woman with a bent back appeared. She hobbled with a cane, the head of which was a dancing skeleton. She motioned for us to follow her. We did not walk long, and soon we were in a graveyard. The old woman led us to two plain gravestones covered with moss. The names of a husband and wife were engraved on the tablets.

"This is where a river comes up every summer," she said. She pointed with her cane to a nearby riverbed with tall banks on either side where a once-strong river had carved its way through the land. "The riverbed is dry now, as you can see, but when the river comes up, it is filled with albino trout. A very rare species. The river flows through underground limestone caverns that are older than time itself, caverns that are said to date to the Garden of Eden. The trout are white because they have spent their lives in darkness."

Franklin studied the names on the gravestones. "Who were they?" he asked.

"A couple from this village who died about ten years ago," the woman said. "The river appeared the night they were buried, and ever since it has flowed between their headstones once a year. The river frightened the other villagers, and they left. I tend the graves."

She continued, "The couple had a son who could neither hear nor speak. They hired a man to take the boy into the forest and leave him to die. The parents changed their minds and went looking for him. The boy was never seen again. He is believed to be dead. They never had children again. They never spoke to anyone after that. They both died of broken hearts on the same day, the anniversary of the day they sent their boy away to die."

When I turned to ask the caretaker a question, she had disappeared. Where to, I had no idea. I would probably never know. But just then I felt the vibration. It seemed to come from the roots of the trees, from somewhere deep in the earth. It rumbled, like an avalanche, a fountain, a bursting dam. All around me was the thundering of rushing water as the river burst from between the headstones and shot between the waiting banks, filling the riverbed with its rolling torrent. We had to climb the tall banks to escape it.

Madeline, Franklin, and I watched the river pour from between the gravestones like a stream of light. The water danced with huge sparks, but when I peered closer I saw that the sparks were actually beautiful white trout. I cut two willow poles with my knife and tied them with horsehair line that I kept in my pocket and then I attached two flies. When the river was about waist-deep, I waded in. Franklin and Madeline followed.

Madeline caught a huge white trout. Its body glowed like the Sun with white scales, and rainbows. The fish had pale eyes that on closer inspection looked like cloud-filled skies. She unhooked the fly and released the fish back into the remarkable river. Franklin, meanwhile, was swimming.

"I feel so good!" he cried. "I feel younger! I wish I knew what was in this water. I would bottle it and give it to everybody I met!"

This was the Brandywine, and it was everything it was supposed to be.

The three of us climbed onto the bank of the river to lie in the sunlight. Where had the time gone? It was almost evening. The Sun was setting, and the Evening Star drifted alone in the dark blue sky. The river was still coursing from between the stones. I noticed that someone else was fishing in the river. He had long black hair and scooped fish out of the water with his bare hands. The fisherman reminded me of White Dog when he had first come to the orphanage. The figure saw me looking at him and waved. I waved back. I stood to get a better look, but then the mist from the rolling water enveloped him. When I looked again, he had vanished into the forest.

There was nothing left to say to Benjamin Franklin except goodbye.

He put his arms around us and wished us Godspeed. Then he packed up his few belongings and said he would head south. By foot, carriage, and boat, taking detours, accidents, and unforeseen circumstances into consideration, he figured it would take him perhaps six weeks to reach New York City.

Madeline and I would begin the long trek back to the orphanage. It was the only home we knew. It would be risky for us, but we would chance it. Perhaps the war would be over by the time we returned.

We were used to sleeping outdoors. Madeline and I would fish and talk, take our time, and gaze at the stars at night. Up there, someday, maybe we would see Franklin again, sailing in his airship, surrounded by electric jars and smoke and sparks.

I had one last look at the Brandywine. The mist had cleared, and in the moonlight the fish were jumping, the unearthly white fish from the timeless caves. Madeline took my hand and smiled.

CHAPTER XX

A Postscript

What you have read up to now is what I wrote when Madeline and I returned to the St. Francis of Assisi Home for Foundlings.

Now we are in Paris. Madeline and I are legally brother and sister. Eliza Fisk adopted me, too. When we made it back to the orphanage, the Rebels were negotiating with the British to exchange Mrs. Fisk for a captured British general who had been taken at a battle near Ticonderoga. As soon as the exchange was made, she took Madeline and me with her to her home in New Haven, Connecticut.

At the end of the year 1776, we were reunited with Ben Franklin and made a dangerous Atlantic crossing on the American warship *Reprisal*. The voyage took six weeks. It was good to see only water and waves and sky. I prefer to look at the sky rather than fly in it. The sky is for birds, not ships. Yet storms followed one after another on the sea and did not let up. I confess there were times when I missed the sky and being so close to the stars.

After our voyage, we waited on the windswept coast of Brittany for several days before anchoring in the little port of Auray. I had expected the British at any moment to swoop down with their frigates and seize us. After all, Franklin is still wanted for treason. At Auray we hired a carriage for Paris — Ville Lumière!

Cook has written me many letters. She says nothing has really changed at the orphanage. Brother Nessus still plays the violoncello furiously and frightens the younger boys and girls. Captain Pennington, however, met a gruesome end. Cook says spirits took revenge upon him for White Dog's death. He was found impaled on his own sword in the entrance to a bear cave some two days' journey from the orphanage. Cook says that Brother Jean honours White Dog by holding chapel outdoors once a month so that the orphans can pray in the sunlight and wind.

I wrote to Cook to ask if she wanted to join us on our voyage across the Atlantic, but she replied that she wanted to stay in the country she knew best and with the spirits who cared for her. Cook said the American army left the plains of Quebec at the end of June 1776. But she said the Rebels continue to fight the British in the Middle Colonies and in the South.

Paris is beautiful and ugly at the same time. The stones in the streets are round and slippery. There are no sidewalks, and when it rains the streets are mud baths. The carriages do not stop for passersby, and one must be careful crossing the street. Madeline and I attend the School for the Deaf founded by the disciples of the Abbé de l'Epée. We are learning so much. Franklin has rented a little house in Passy, just outside Paris. His job in Paris is to secure France's alliance while the war with Britain is waged. It will not be easy. The agents of the British Secret Service have been sent to France to thwart his efforts.

Franklin is using our dictionary more than ever. I have also proposed a combination code using home-sign symbols with a grid. In this method, messages are read through a mask or grille. This is known as the Cardan system, named after Gerolamo Cardano, a famous Italian code-maker and mathematician of the sixteenth century.

Today Mother and Madeline have gone shopping. Franklin is having lunch with the Montgolfier brothers, who are interested in hearing about Franklin's flying machine.

Franklin's patriotic duty is clear: to help win the war against Great Britain, the most powerful nation on Earth. To do this he will have to survive the net of spies that has been thrown around him. I am determined to root out these spies wherever they are. I will travel silently, like a shadow. They will neither see nor hear me. I will help Franklin win his war or my name is not Michael Flynn — spy, writer, and fly-fisherman of Quebec and the World.

FURTHER READING

Becker, Carl L. *Benjamin Franklin: A Biographical Sketch.* Ithaca, NY: Cornell University Press, 1946.

Commager, Henry Steele. *The Autobiography of Benjamin Franklin.* New York: The Modern Library, 1944.

Currey, Cecil B. *Code Number 72: Ben Franklin Patriot or Spy?* Englewood Cliffs, NJ: Prentice-Hall, 1972.

____. *Road to Revolution.* New York: Doubleday, 1968.

Ellet, Elizabeth F. *The Women of the American Revolution.* Volumes 1, 2, and 3. New York: Haskell House Publishers, 1850; reprinted 1969.

Ford, Paul Leicester. *The Many-Sided Franklin.* Freeport, NY: Books for Libraries Press, 1898; reprinted 1972.

Franklin, Benjamin. *The Complete Poor Richard's Almanack.* Volume 1, 1733–1747; Volume 2, 1748–1758. Barre, MA: The Imprint Society, 1970.

Hornberger, Theodore. *Benjamin Franklin: Pamphlets on American Writers*. Number 19. Minneapolis: University of Minnesota Press, 1962.

Labaree, Leonard, Ralph Ketcham, Helen Boatfield, and Helene Fineman, eds. *The Autobiography of Benjamin Franklin*. New Haven, CT: Yale University Press, 1964.

Lane, Harlan. *The Wild Boy of Aveyron*. Cambridge, MA: Harvard University Press, 1976.

_____. *When the Mind Hears*. New York: Random House, 1984.

Lopez, Claude-Anne. *Mon Cher Papa and the Ladies of Paris*. New Haven, CT: Yale University Press, 1966.

Mascall, Leonard. *A Booke of Fishing with Hooke & Line*. New York: Da Capo Press, 1973; originally published in 1590.

Ryan, Dennis P., ed. *A Salute to Courage: The American Revolution as Seen Through Wartime Writings of Officers of the Continental Army and Navy*. New York: Columbia University Press, 1979.

Trigger, Bruce G. *Children of Aataentsic: A History of the Huron People to 1660*. Kingston and Montreal: McGill-Queen's University Press, 1987.

U.S. National Archives. *The Formation of the Union: A Documentary History Based upon an Exhibit in the National Archives.* Washington, D.C.: U.S. National Archives, 1970.

Van Doren, Carl. *Benjamin Franklin's Autobiographical Writings.* New York: Viking, 1945.

Walton, Izaak. *The Compleat Angler, 1653–1676.* Oxford: Clarendon Press, 1983.

Walton, Izaak, and Charles Cotton. *The Compleat Angler.* London: Oxford University Press, 1960.

White, James. *A New Century of Inventions.* New York: Burt Franklin, 1822.

Zall, P.M., ed. *Ben Franklin Laughing: Anecdotes from Original Sources by and About Benjamin Franklin.* Berkeley, CA: University of California Press, 1980.